D1454830

A NEW LOOK
AT 16TH-CENTURY
COUNTERPOINT

Margarita Merriman
Atlantic Union College

UNIVERSITY
PRESS OF
AMERICA

LANHAM • NEW YORK • LONDON

Copyright © 1982 by

University Press of America,™ Inc.

4720 Boston Way
Lanham, MD 20706

3 Henrietta Street
London WC2E 8LU England

Library of Congress Cataloging in Publication Data

Merriman, Margarita.
 A new look at 16th-century counterpoint.

 1. Counterpoint. I. Title. II. Title: A new look at
sixteenth-century counterpoint.
MT55.M575   781.4'2   81–40924
ISBN 0–8191–2391–9
ISBN 0–8191–2392–7 (pbk.)

DEDICATION

To the memory of my teacher, Gustave
Soderlund; to the many aspiring contrapuntalists who have survived my classes; and
to future students for whom the road to
contrapuntal skill may be a bit smoother.

iv

Table of Contents

Preface

APPENDIX

A NEW LOOK AT SIXTEENTH CENTURY COUNTERPOINT

PREFACE

In an era when each composer is free to write his own rules or choose from a plethora of styles, a blank sheet of staff paper can utterly intimidate the novice. It is when the dry well of inspiration is in need of priming that the greatest demands are made upon pure craftsmanship. Fortunately, craftsmanship can be taught.

The study of Renaissance sacred counterpoint, as exemplified in the style of Palestrina and others, is still rewarding. As a discipline, it is a beneficial counterpoise to twentieth-century freedom. As a primarily linear art, it places stress upon interaction of melodies while minimizing chordal function, and thus is more akin to twentieth-century practice than is the chord-oriented counterpoint of the Baroque period.

It was said of Josquin, the greatest master of the early Renaissance: "He is the master of the notes. They must do as he wills; as for the other composers, they have to do as the notes will."[1]

Such mastery does not come primarily by inspiration. Combining notes into phrases and phrases into compositions is a craft and, as such, must be practiced assiduously if it is to be perfected. Bach's high regard for diligence is apparent from his unduly modest statement: "I was obliged to be industrious; whoever is equally industrious will succeed equally well."[2]

While the study of sixteenth-century counterpoint will not necessarily produce a modern Josquin or Bach, it will certainly reward the persistent. In a style where every note requires a raison d'être, the successful contrapuntalist is an expert problem solver.

[1] Donald J. Grout, A History of Western Music, revised, p. 195.

[2] Hans T. David and Arthur Mendel, The Bach Reader, p. 334.

Throughout the Middle Ages music was taught as a branch of mathematics, and in actuality, the mentalities of the mathematician and the composer are similar.

The sixteenth century has been aptly called "the golden age of polyphony." While we laud the composers of sacred music, most notably Palestrina, for their unrivaled mystical qualities and their perfection within a highly restricted idiom, we must not ignore the contributions of the madrigalists and other secular composers whose daring harmonic experiments, when viewed in historical perspective, are of tremendous importance. The Palestrina style is notable for its consistency, the madrigal style for its audacity.

This book does not claim to enlarge upon the research of Jeppesen, Morris, Soderlund, and others who have treated the Palestrina style in a thorough and scholarly manner. But there seems to be a dearth of textbooks that organize this body of knowledge into units suitable for classroom use. Also, it is felt that since most students are comfortable with only the treble and bass clefs, the various movable clefs that appear in some textbooks are best avoided.

Previous mastery of music fundamentals is assumed. Some knowledge of harmony is beneficial but not essential. The assignments at the end of each chapter are suggestive and can be abridged or expanded.

The species approach is here abandoned as being pedantic and unmusical. From the first, the student is encouraged to make his exercises as artistic as possible, and, since sixteenth-century polyphony is a vocal art, the student will be setting words almost from the beginning. Admittedly, text setting creates some hazards, but it gives a practical dimension to the study. Traditional Latin texts, English translations, sacred and secular verse are suggested options, though the student is free to select his own words.

It is hoped that the student can relate his "problem solving" to "music making" in such a manner that his best homework will not find its way into the trash can, but will be retained as a resource upon which he may draw in the future, whether as composer, performer, or choral director.

CHAPTER ONE: MELODY

Counterpoint is the art of combining melodic lines. Polyphony is a synonym which tends to refer primarily to that great flowering of unaccompanied choral music in the sixteenth century. Counterpoint is presumed to have had its genesis in Europe in the ninth century, and has ever since been a prominent feature of western music. It developed in the church and derived its early sustenance from the chants which constituted much of the liturgy.

The sacred polyphony of the Renaissance, like that of the Middle Ages, was firmly rooted in Gregorian chant. A particular chant (also known as plainsong or plainchant) might serve as the borrowed melody (cantus firmus) upon which an individual composition was based, but, more often, the sixteenth-century composer wrote melodies infused with the spirit of Gregorian chant.

No description of plainsong can substitute for the aural experience of hearing it sung in its proper setting. Where no such opportunity exists, recorded performances can give a semblance of the mystical elevation of spirit provided by a cathedral worship service. The student can also profitably sing examples from the many available chant collections.

Features of Gregorian chant shared by sixteenth-century melody are subtlety, modality, free rhythm, narrow range, and basically stepwise motion punctuated by narrow skips. The guidelines that follow should be carefully observed by the student even though occasional lapses may be encountered in various Renaissance choral compositions.

USE OF MODES

There were twelve modes used in vocal polyphony, but since the distinction between the authentic and the plagal forms depended solely upon range, for practical purposes there were only six. The numbering system applies also to Gregorian chant, and in chant books is used instead of the modal names. The relation between authentic and plagal modes is similar to that between soprano and alto in a hymn or part song. (For example, in "Before Jehovah's Awful Throne" the soprano range

1

is d' to d" while the alto range is a to f#', yet both are in D major.

It was often impossible to determine the mode of a piece until the final cadence. Terms like "tonic" and "keynote" are not applicable to Gregorian chant or Renaissance polyphony since functional harmony did not develop until the Baroque period. Hence, the term "final" refers to the last note of a chant or the last bass note of a polyphonic work. In the following chart the final of each mode is shown as a white note.

Example 1 - 1

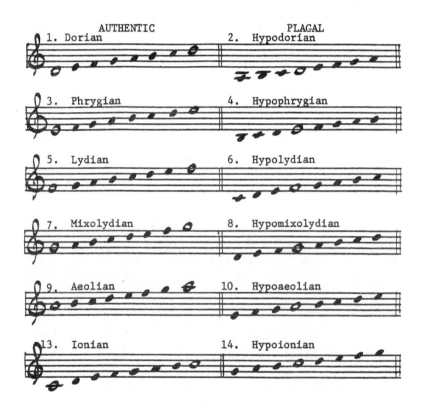

The eleventh and twelfth modes, called Locrian and Hypolocrian, exist theoretically, but are not practical since a triad erected on the note B is diminished.

Twentieth-century composers utilizing the modes
readily transpose them to any pitch, using either the
signature which corresponds to the scale or the signature of the major or minor key which is most similar.
It is readily apparent that the Dorian, Phrygian, and
Aeolian modes are basically minor, whereas the Lydian,
Mixolydian, and Ionian relate to the major. In the
Renaissance, however, only the transposition down a
perfect fifth was possible with the resulting signature
of one flat. Generally, the modes appeared in their
untransposed form.

Accidentals were used experimentally in the sixteenth century by the madrigalists. On the other hand,
the conservative church composers, most notably Palestrina, used accidentals for color very sparingly. The
only possible sharps were F, C, and G, and these were
used primarily at cadences to create leading tones in
those modes where they were lacking. A tritone (augmented fourth or diminished fifth) was corrected by
the use of B♭, which in a transposed mode would become
E♭.[1]

While a melody normally ended on the final, the
beginning note could be the final or the pitch a perfect fifth above the final. In the Phrygian mode, A
was also used used as a starting note. Interior cadences could occur on pitches other than the final of
the mode. However, E was used very rarely except in
the Phrygian mode, F occurred primarily in the Lydian
and Dorian modes, and B was never used as a cadence
point.

RHYTHM

The rhythm of Gregorian chant was based on Bibli-
cal prose. It was free and irregular. Polyphony likewise had irregular groupings in individual parts, with
special care being taken to distribute the agogic accents (stress resulting from long notes) so that the
stress shifted from one voice part to another.

[1]A tritone involving prominent pitches was often
corrected, even where one or two pitches separated the
offending tones, as when a tritone involved high and
low points of the phrase, long notes, or the last note
of a phrase.

Example 1 - 2

It should be borne in mind that barlines did not come into use until the close of the sixteenth century. There was, however, a gentle alternation of strong and weak pulses, determined not by dynamic accentuation but by distribution of consonance and varying degrees of dissonance.

White notation was generally used in polyphony. The following values were possible:

Maxima	(equivalent to 8 whole notes)	
Longa	(equivalent to 4 whole notes)	
Brevis	(double whole note)	
Semibreve	(whole note)	
Minim	(half note)	
Crotchet	(quarter note)	
Quaver	(eighth note)	

Since in modern editions barlines are used with a signature of ₵, representing $\frac{4}{2}$, values longer than the brevis are accomplished by the use of ties.

Any of the above values could be dotted, with the exception of the eighth note. Equal white values were tied, or white values could be tied to half their value (corresponding to a dotted note). Dotted whole notes occurred only on strong beats (1 or 3).

Occasionally a passage in triple time occurred with a signature of 𝇲 which would translate into $\frac{3}{1}$ or $\frac{3}{2}$.

4

In many modern editions the note values are
halved, presumably because of the tendency of perform-
ers to associate white notation with a slow tempo.
Also, modern editions sometimes use transpositions not
allowed in the sixteenth-century because of the high
tessitura (placement of the majority of the notes) of
much Renaissance polyphony. It is generally not difficult to detect which editions have altered the note
values. A preponderance of quarter notes and meters
$\frac{4}{4}$ or $\frac{3}{4}$ indicate the values are halved. Throughout this
text white notation is retained. However, both types
of notation are encountered in the compositions for
analysis in the Appendix.

SKIPS

In polyphony, as in Gregorian chant, predominantly
stepwise melodic movement was interrupted by skips of
thirds, fourths, or fifths, either ascending or descending. Sixths were infrequent and used only in ascending form. In polyphony, octave leaps occurred
occasionally, either ascending or descending. Augmented, diminished, and chromatic intervals were not
used.

Skips tended to be approached and left in a direction opposite to the skip. This was especially
true of skips of a fifth, a sixth, or an octave.

Example 1 - 3

Two skips in the same direction generally outlined
major or minor triads or their inversions. They were
usually approached and left by contrary motion. Occasionally, an ascending fifth was followed by a minor
third, especially in the Dorian mode.

Example 1 - 4

5

PHRASES

The student will find the following observations helpful:

1. The first phrase of a composition always begins on beat one with at least a dotted half note value. Subsequent phrases may begin on any beat.

2. In a true cadence the last note arrives on a strong beat and is at least a whole note value. Punctuation by rests of at least a half note value is required between phrases and sometimes interrupts a phrase where the text permits.

3. Phrases of varying lengths are desirable, though short phrases are rare. It should be borne in mind that vocal polyphony must make allowance for breathing.

4. Because of the prevalence of suspensions at the cadence, the final note of a phrase is best approached stepwise. When approached from below, the penultimate note is characteristically a half note preceded by a long note (such as a whole note or tied halves). When approached from above, the penultimate note is a whole note.

5. All cadences except the Phrygian are approached from below by a half step. This will necessitate the use of a sharped F, C, and G. All cadences except the Phrygian are approached from above by a whole step. Except in the case of the Phrygian cadence on A, the note which descends stepwise to the cadence will require no accidental. In the following example (a) and (c) require no accidentals, (b) and (d) require raised leading tones, and (e) requires a B^b to create a Phrygian cadence on A.

Example 1 - 5

RANGE

Characteristically, Renaissance tessitura (especially in the tenor) was high. However, for practical reasons it would be well for the student to restrict the voice parts to ranges considered normal for the average amateur chorus, keeping the tessitura toward the middle of the range. The following suggested ranges indicate tessitura in black notes.

Example 1 - 6

ASSIGNMENTS

1. Sing each authentic mode till it feels natural.
2. Sing the examples of Gregorian chant found in the Appendix. If it is necessary to use an instrument as a crutch, repeat unaccompanied.
3. Sing duets by Lassus (Appendix, pp. 117-122) with a partner or play one line while singing the other.
4. Determine the agogic accents in a polyphonic work (e.g. Appendix, pp. 159-162) and note how the emphasis shifts from one voice to another, as well as the irregular grouping of beats from one accent to the next.

5. Write phrases as follows employing only white notes and paying special attention to irregular placement of agogic accents:

   a) Soprano--Dorian
   b) Alto--Phrygian
   c) Tenor[2]--Lydian
   d) Bass--Mixolydian

6. Write a three-phrase melody (white notes only) beginning and ending on A with internal cadences on D and C.

[2]For tenor use either 𝄢 or 𝄞𝄞 clef.

CHAPTER TWO: TEXT SETTING

Counterpoint was born and nurtured in the church. From Guido in the eleventh century to Machaut, who in the fourteenth century composed the first complete polyphonic Mass, the roster of medieval composers contributing to contrapuntal development is made up of men devoted to the service of God.

By the time of the Renaissance, contrapuntal techniques were shared by both sacred and secular forms. Most composers of Dufay's generation were equally at home writing Masses, motets, and chansons. Later composers tended to specialize, though the versatile Orlandus Lassus was a notable exception. But not only did polyphonic art expand to include secular vocal forms. Instrumental music began its long development by imitating the motet and the chanson. Clearly, polyphony had matured and moved out of the church.

The Renaissance was a period of experimentation. The rise of instrumental music, the growth of virtuoso ornamentation, the chromatic harmonies of the late madrigalists, as well as overpowering polychoral effects, all served to undermine the basis of sacred polyphony which, in the hands of the Flemish masters, had represented the classical ideals of restraint and balance. By the mid-fifteenth century the Council of Trent, alarmed at various abuses in the Roman Church, decreed that church music should be purged of secular associations and that the words should be clearly understood.

At about this time Palestrina was perfecting his style which was to become the epitome of sixteenth-century sacred polyphony. As a reactionary style that chose to ignore the developments of the madrigalists and other progressives, it was a perfect vehicle for the Counter-Reformation search for a mystical man-God relationship. As an unusually consistent style, it was used throughout coming generations as the basis for the study of the counterpoint of the "Golden Age" and a yardstick by which new works could be measured.

Since Palestrina's art was a purely vocal one, any attempt to imitate his style must involve text setting. And since he was concerned almost exclusively with writing for the church, his style lends itself much

better to sacred than to secular texts. Whether the
imitator chooses to use Latin or English, it should be
obvious that Latin produces not only a more musical,
but a more authentic sound. However, for practical
reasons the student should learn to set English as well.
And, when the problems of text setting are mastered, he
should be permitted the freedom of writing for instru-
ments since they were normally used to double and substitute for voice parts in Renaissance polyphony.

RULES FOR TEXT SETTING

Rules for text setting were formulated by Vicentino
and Zarlino in the sixteenth century and were based upon the common practice of the period. They can be ap-
plied to any language.

The student should, for the time being, restrict
his values to white notes. This considerably reduces
the chances of awkwardness in text setting. Additional
rules will be added when quarter and eighth notes are
incorporated, but for the present the following will
suffice:

1. Word accents should coincide with agogic and
   metrical accents in the music.
2. Repeated notes require separate syllables.
   (Ornamental quarter notes will later constitute
   an exception.)
3. Where there is imitation of one voice by another, the text setting of the first appearance
   must be maintained.
4. The final note of a musical phrase demands a
   syllable.

The student should sing each phrase as he finishes
it. If any awkwardness is felt, the phrase should be
reconstructed. Palestrina's style is characterized by
extreme smoothness and restrained emotion.

For the present the student should limit himself to
the ₵ (⁴₂) signature most typical of the style. He
should also notice that notes on or above the middle
line have downward stems, while those below the middle
line require upward stems.

ASSIGNMENTS:

1. Sing phrases from Palestrina Masses and motets (see Appendix), noting especially the placement of syllables.

2. Make melodic settings for the following texts:
   a) Miserere nobis
   b) Have mercy upon us
   c) The Lord is my shepherd

3. Set a text of your choosing.

CHAPTER THREE: CONSONANCE

Counterpoint and harmony differ primarily in emphasis. In true counterpoint melodies create chords, while in harmony chords dictate the movement of individual voice lines. Except at cadences Renaissance counterpoint was basically linear and unconcerned with chord progressions. But during the Baroque period counterpoint became a slave to chordal function with the result that the dividing line between harmony and counterpoint became blurred.

While the horizontal line is of primary concern to the student of modal counterpoint, the vertical aspect must always be considered. Consonances may occur on any beat, while dissonances must be carefully regulated. The intervals accepted as consonances are the unison, major and minor thirds, the perfect fifth, major and minor sixths, and the octave. The perfect fourth is considered consonant only under certain conditions in textures of three or more parts. Compound intervals (intervals greater than an octave) are permissable, but in two parts are used sparingly.

The following rules governing movement from one interval to the next should be mastered:

1) Parallel perfect intervals (unisons, fifths, and octaves) are forbidden.
2) Unisons on strong beats occur only at the beginning and end of the phrase.[1] They are approached or left by contrary motion.
3) Unisons may occur on weak beats if they are approached by oblique motion (one part holding).

Example 3 - 1

[1]Exceptions do occur in Josquin des Prez and others, but by the late Renaissance unisons on strong beats were rare within a phrase.

13

4) Octaves and fifths may be approached by contrary or oblique motion.

5) Hidden fifths and octaves occur when an interval approaches a fifth or an octave in similar motion. Hidden octaves are forbidden, but fifths may occasionally be approached in similar motion by step in the upper voice and skip in the lower.

Example 3 - 2

6) Two perfect intervals on successive strong beats are avoided.

Example 3 - 3

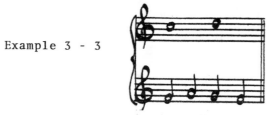

7) Parallel thirds and sixths should be limited to three in succession when using white note values because prolonged parallelism involving any interval destroys linear independence.

The time-honored species approach to the study of counterpoint has the advantage of simplicity, but since it ignores aesthetic considerations, it has more value for the problem solver than for the aspiring composer. The following are correct but uninspired:

First species (note against note; even values)

Example 3 - 4

14

Second species (two notes against one; even values)

Example 3 - 5

The third species consists of four quarter notes against each whole note, the fourth species involves the use of ties, and the fifth species is free. Obviously, the first four species create artificial music which bears little resemblance to actual compositions.

The following assignments involve some aesthetic considerations. It is suggested that the student write without aid of an instrument, but that, upon completion of an exercise, he play each part while singing the other to check both sound and ease of performance.

ASSIGNMENTS:

Write each part upon a separate staff giving consideration to melodic independence. Write for adjacent voices in modes of your choosing. Always mark the intervals, using only consonances at present. Begin on a unison, fifth, or on an octave. End on a unison or an octave, remembering the stepwise approach to the cadence note.[2] For the first two assignments a solution is given.

1) Compose a note against note setting similar to the following, in unequal values, of a three-fold Amen.[3]

[2]This type of cadence is referred to as the clausula vera.

[3]Notice that it is not possible to approach the final by a descent from a whole note and an ascent from a half note here. If the C# is delayed by one beat, a suspension typical of the style will result.

15

2) Compose a phrase similar to the following for two rhythmically independent voices.

3) Add a soprano voice above this <u>cantus</u> <u>firmus</u>.

4) Add a tenor voice below this <u>cantus</u> <u>firmus</u>.

CHAPTER FOUR: DISSONANCE

In the Palestrina style dissonance was carefully controlled. Nonharmonic devices occurring in the style were limited to passing tones, suspensions, neighboring tones, the portamento, and the Nota Cambiata. On strong beats (one and three in $\frac{4}{2}$ time) the only possible dissonance was the suspension. On the other two beats half-note passing tones were allowed to ascend or descend, but quarter-note passing tones could only descend. Permissible on the second half of any beat were ascending and descending passing tones, lower and (rarely) upper neighboring tones, and the escape tone of the Nota Cambiata. The portamento in both its consonant and dissonant forms was restricted to the second half of beats one and three.

For practical reasons the discussion of nonharmonic devices employing quarter notes will be deferred to a later chapter. For the present the student will find sufficient challenge in dealing with half-note passing tones and the types of suspension suitable to two-part counterpoint.

HALF-NOTE PASSING TONES

A passing tone is a nonharmonic (dissonant) tone approached and left by step in a scalewise motion. In the Palestrina style it is always diatonic. It can be either accented or unaccented. A half-note passing tone on a weak beat is considered unaccented and occurs against a note already sounding which, for the present, should be at least a whole note. (A quarter-note passing tone is considered accented if it falls on a beat and unaccented if it does not.) Though the passing tone is approached and left by step, the note opposite it may skip to a consonance.

The following example illustrates both ascending and descending passing tones. The tritone is acceptable because of its nonharmonic status.

17

Example 4 - 1

In the next example note the following:

(a)   Correct but consonant and therefore not a
      passing tone
(b)   Wrong beat
(c)   Incorrect because the harmony should not
      have changed

Example 4 - 2

SUSPENSIONS

The suspension is the most common and striking non-harmonic device used in the sixteenth century. It involves a consonant note which is retained to form a dissonance before it is resolved downward by step to a consonance.

The suspension always requires at least three full beats in the Palestrina style. The preparation takes place on a weak beat, the suspension dissonance is given added poignancy and prominence by falling on a strong beat, and the downward resolution on the following beat releases the tension. Both the preparation

and the resolution may be longer than one beat, but the
suspension itself is limited to one beat. The resolution of one suspension may form the preparation of another. In a string of suspensions usually at least one
is ornamented. (Ornamental resolutions will be studied
later.)

Though they may occur anywhere in the phrase, suspensions are typically found at cadences with the note
of resolution leading upward to the final cadence point.

The only suspensions which are practical in two-
part polyphony are the 7-6 and its inversion, the 2-3.
In three or more parts the 4-3, the 9-8 (2-1) and double suspensions are also available. The 2-3 suspension
is in the lowest voice, while all others involve the
upper voices.

The following example illustrates correct uses of
the suspension device:

Example 4 - 3

Common errors are illustrated below:

(a) Suspension attempted on a weak beat
(b) Dissonant preparation
(c) Less than three beats
(d) 2-3 in upper voice, upward resolution

Example 4 - 4

19

ASSIGNMENTS:

1. Compose short two-part excerpts illustrating passing tones. Involve each dissonant interval and
   place the passing tones in both upper and lower
   voices.
2. Rewrite the following cadences to create suspensions.
   a) For the 7-6 suspension
   b) For the 2-3 suspension

3. Locate suspensions in two-part works.[1] Note frequency, placement in the phrase, ornamental resolutions, length of preparation.
4. Compose phrases as follows:
   a) An internal 7-6 suspension with a 2-3 at the
      cadence.
   b) An internal 2-3 suspension with a 7-6 at the
      cadence.
5. Compose a phrase making use of both passing tones
   and suspensions.
6. Set the following texts as effectively as possible
   for rhythmically independent voices:
   a) Kyrie eleison
   b) Behold, the Lamb of God

[1]See Appendix, pp. 117-124. The works by Lassus
use white notation, whereas the note values are halved
in the other example.

CHAPTER FIVE: IMITATION

Imitation involves a restatement in one voice of a melody (theme or subject) which has previously appeared in another voice. The imitation may be above the original voice or below it, an exact copy or a slightly altered version. The pitch level of the imitation may or may not be the same as that of the original statement. Though any diatonic interval relationship between the two appearances of a melody is possible, adjacant voices normally imitate at the interval of a fourth or fifth.

In strict imitation the leader (also referred to as Dux or antecedent) is copied note by note without rhythmic or intervallic change by the follower (also called Comes or consequent). While the intervals retain their numerical relationship, the quality may change as dictated by the scale or mode. (For example, a major third in the leader may become a minor third in the follower.)

Example 5 - 1

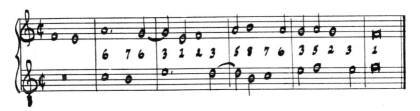

Strict imitation continued throughout a composition is known as canon and dates back to the thirteenth century. In multivoiced compositions all voices may participate in the canon (as in a round), or one or more voices may be independent.

In free imitation only the beginning of a theme is answered note for note, and the composer is then free to complete the phrase as he wishes. Compositions of the sixteenth century typically begin each new phrase with a point of imitation in which all voices participate before going their own ways.

Example 5 - 2

Free imitation may be either real or tonal. In real imitation the theme is answered without intervallic change, whereas in tonal imitation adjustments are made to preserve a feeling of tonality.[1] Since in the sixteenth century tonality was vague, composers tended to prefer real answers. As tonality developed during the Baroque period, composers found tonal imitation to be a necessity in certain instances.[2]

DEVICES

Technical devices applicable to both strict and free imitation are inversion (mirroring), augmentation, diminution, cancrizans (recte et retro), and stretto. Such feats of skill were common with Flemish composers of the fifteenth century, such as Ockeghem, but were used to a lesser degree by church composers of the Renaissance. They again appear in the late Baroque,[3] in scattered works of the Classical period,[4] and they are basic to the serial technique of the twentieth century. The devices may be used singly or in combination.

Each device is described and illustrated below. The wavy lines indicate the extent of the imitation.

[1]See Appendix, pp. 119-120. Phrases one and three illustrate real and tonal imitation, respectively.

[2]See Bach Well-tempered Clavier Vol. I, Fugues 2,3, 7,8,11-13,16-19,21-24.

[3]Notably in the masterful "Art of Fugue" and "Musical Offering" by J. S. Bach.

[4]E.g., F. J. Haydn's "Ten Commandments".

22

<u>Inversion</u> (mirroring).

The ascending or descending movement of one voice
is imitated by reversing the motion in another voice
while (usually) retaining the numerical value of the
intervals.

Example 5 - 3

In the following quotation from a Magnificat by
Palestrina the alto mirrors the soprano and the bass
mirrors the tenor.[5]

Example 5 - 4

<u>Augmentation.</u>

The note values of the leader are consistently
doubled (sometimes tripled or quadrupled) in the
followers.

[5]See Appendix, pp. 134-135 for the entire section.

Example 5 - 5

In the following five-part Agnus Dei by Palestrina, Tenor II doubles the values of Tenor I. [6] The augmentation continues throughout the movement.

Example 5 - 6

Diminution.

The note values of the leader are consistently reduced (usually halved) so that the follower soon becomes the leader. This device is rare in Palestrina though the initial note of a theme is often lengthened or shortened. Also, the contour of a theme may be retained while the rhythm is altered. [7]

[6] See Appendix, pp. 179-181.
[7] See Appendix, p.199 for rhythmic variations.

Example 5 - 7

Cancrizans.

The translation of cancrizans is "crab", and refers
to that crustacean's reputed ability to move backwards.
In cancrizans the theme is reversed. This device can
be detected visually, but is hardly noticeable aurally
and hence is of questionable musical value. Cancrizans
is almost impossible to accomplish in sixteenth-century
style unless consonances occur on each beat or one al-
lows some rhythmic freedom.

Example 5 - 8

Stretto.

Stretto involves imitation delayed by a very short
time interval. In the Baroque period it is apt to be
used to build a climax near the close of a fugue.
Stretto delayed by only one beat is not very practical
in sixteenth-century style because of problems encountered with the handling of dissonance.

Example 5 - 9

25

PROCEDURE

When a phrase commences on a strong beat, the imitation will usually (except in stretto) also begin on a strong beat. Likewise, leader and follower correspond when the phrase begins on a weak beat. This arrangement facilitates the proper placement of suspensions, passing tones, and other nonharmonic devices.

The text setting should be identical in each appearance for the duration of the imitation. Since after each point of imitation the counterpoint usually becomes free, the text setting will correspond only at the beginning of each phrase with the last syllable of text being reserved for the final cadence note.

Imitation is accomplished by composing the leader up to the point where the imitation begins. The follower copies the leader at the desired pitch level. Then a counterpoint is added until the leader "catches up," at which time the follower copies the new material. This process continues for the duration of the imitation. In free imitation the imitation will cease before the end of the phrase.

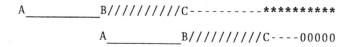

ASSIGNMENTS:

1. Mark all the points of imitation in the Kyrie found on pp. 139-143 of the Appendix. Notice the duration of each restatement and the nature of the liberties taken by Palestrina.
2. Find the interval at which strict imitation is possible and copy the follower which will begin at x.

3. Compose examples using real imitation for at least three measures before permitting the follower to become free.
   a) Imitate at the fourth above.
   b) Imitate at the third below.
   c) Imitate at the unison.
4. Compose examples with slight intervallic or rhythmic adjustments.
   a) Imitate at the fifth above.
   b) Imitate at the sixth below.
5. Write a phrase to illustrate each of the following:
   a) Inversion
   b) Augmentation
   c) Diminution
6. For a greater challenge, attempt the following:
   a) Cancrizans
   b) Stretto involving a delay of one beat
7. Set texts making sure the syllabic treatment is identical in leader and follower.

CHAPTER SIX: BLACK NOTES IN A MELODIC LINE

The only black note values in general use in the
sixteenth century were the quarter note and the eighth
note. A quick survey of Palestrina compositions in the
Appendix will reveal a sprinkling of quarter notes on
most pages. Eighth notes are rare and are almost always
found in pairs. [1] Quarter and eighth rests do not occur
in the style.

THE NOTA CAMBIATA

A distinctive sixteenth century melodic idiom is
the Nota Cambiata. [2] It is a four-note figure consisting
of a downward step, a downward leap of a third, and a
stepwise rise. Of the following rhythmic forms, the
first is most frequent:

Example 6 - 1

These also occur with doubled values in fast triple
time. The Nota Cambiata can begin on any beat. When
it starts on beat four, it will be tied across the bar-
line. The final note of the Cambiata may be extended
in value. Unless it is the final note of the composition, the fourth note is generally followed by an ascending step. The Cambiata is used effectively at a
final cadence, in which case a chromatic inflection may
be necessary.

STEPWISE QUARTER NOTES IN THE MELODIC LINE

Quarter notes occur in scale passages where they
are preceded and followed by white notes with no change

---

[1] This would not be true of editions in which the
note values have been halved.

[2] Literally "changed note." A note which started
as a passing tone is exchanged for a note a third lower
before it resolves.

of direction. They may number from one to ten, though
extensive scale passages are not typical.

Since syncopation involving a fraction of a beat is
foreign to the style, a white note following a quarter
note passage always occurs on a beat. A dotted half
value is used to precede an odd number of quarter notes.
A dotted half is never followed by a rest.

Example 6 - 2

Pairs of quarter notes are usually found on weak
beats except when used to lead into a Cambiata or suspension figure. When preceded by a value longer than
a half note, a pair of quarter notes generally descends.
In the following example (a) shows normal treatment and
(b) and (c) are acceptable, while (d) and (e) are unacceptable.

Example 6 - 3

An interior phrase may now begin with a dotted half
note. Interior phrases may also begin with a quarter
note passage of at least four notes. The number will
be even since the phrase must begin on a beat and a
half note is never split between two beats.

A change of direction may occur before, during, or
after a quarter note passage. The general tendency is
to avoid having the high point of a phrase fall on the
off beat. Consequently, (a) is to be preferred over
(b), though there is no strict prohibition of the latter.

Example 6 - 4

30

SKIPS INVOLVING QUARTER NOTES

Skips from half notes to quarter note passages are
common. As before, after a large skip a change of
direction is desirable. When quarter notes are left
by skip, there is always a change of direction except
in the Cambiata figure. Correct usage is illustrated
by the following example.

Example 6 - 5

Skips involving quarter notes are subject to the
"high note law" which permits only descending skips
within a beat. An ascending skip which places an agogic accent on an off-beat creates a mild syncopation
which is incompatible with the Palestrina style. In
the following example (a) and (b) are correct while
(c) and (d) violate the high note law.

Example 6 - 6

Consecutive quarter note skips in the same direction
are very rare. A white note skip may be followed by a
skip to a black note passage provided the two skips out-
line a triad, an inversion of a triad, or an octave with
intervening fourth or fifth. A change of direction will
begin with the quarter note passage.

Example 6 - 7

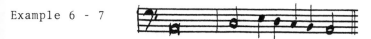

Consecutive quarter note skips with change of direction are permissible if the high note law is not viola-
ted. Also, a skip involving quarter notes may be followed by a skip in the opposite direction to a white
note.

Example 6 - 8

Sequences are rare in Palestrina and should be avoided by the student.[3]

EIGHTH NOTES

Eighth notes usually occur in pairs found on the second half of the beat. They are approached and left by stepwise motion. They appear as passing tones and neighboring tones with the lower neighbor being more common than the upper neighbor. Eighth notes are ornamental and are used sparingly in the sixteenth century.

Example 6 - 9

TIES AND REPEATED NOTES

Half notes may be tied to quarter notes (corresponding to the dot), but quarter notes are rarely tied to one another as this would create syncopation. Eighth notes are never involved in ties in the style.

Repeated quarter notes are used principally in the portamento figure which will be discussed in a later chapter. In syllabic, declamatory text setting quarter notes may be repeated. Some motets treat the text in this manner, though typically Palestrina style is neither syllabic nor declamatory.

TEXT SETTING

In general, only white notes can be assigned a syllable. A melismatic (florid) passage must complete a syllable with a white note before a new syllable is begun.

Example 6 - 10

[3]See Appendix, p. 203.

Exceptions are as follows:
1. An accented syllable followed by two unaccented syllables (Domine, Kyrie, sapientia) may be set by a dotted half followed by a quarter and a white value (𝅗𝅥. 𝅘𝅥 𝅗𝅥).

Example 6 - 11

Do- mi- ne Oc-   us.

2. A syllable may be assigned to a passage of at least four quarter notes within a phrase or at the beginning of a phrase. The syllable comes at the start of the passage and must begin on a beat.

Example 6 - 12

om-   ni- po- ten-   tum.

   The last note of a phrase usually takes a new syllable. Since the passage must reach a white note before changing syllables, the final two notes will both be white values. It will be noted that the typical Palestrina phrase gathers momentum in the middle and slows to a stop.

ASSIGNMENTS

1. Locate seven Cambiata figures on pp. 205-207 of the Appendix noting starting beats and rhythmic forms.
2. Describe the errors identified in the following melody. Remember that the rules given in earlier chapters are still in effect.

33

3. Write extended phrases (six to nine measures) in-corporating quarter notes and an occasional eighth note pair. White notes should still predominate in actual time value though not necessarily in number of notes. (The alleluia in the section on text setting has eleven beats assigned to white notes and five involving quarters. However, only seven of the sixteen notes are white).
4. Set the following texts melodically:
   a) Magnificat anima mea Dominum
   b) My soul doth magnify the Lord
   c) Exaltabo te, Domine
   d) I will exalt Thee, O Lord

CHAPTER SEVEN: COUNTERPOINT USING ALL NOTE VALUES

The addition of black note values frees the contra-puntalist to use a wider variety of nonharmonic devices. Whereas only the suspension and passing tone dissonances have been available heretofore, it is now possible to incorporate neighboring tones, the escape tone as found in the Nota Cambiata, and the anticipation as it occurs in the portamento figure. The new freedom presents new hazards, however, for the novice. It is essential that the student memorize which devices are permissible on what beats or fraction of a beat. Just as the suspension is relegated to beats one and three and the half-note passing tone to beats two and four, each nonharmonic device has its appropriate rhythmic location.

NEIGHBORING TONES[1]

A neighboring tone is a dissonant note approached by step and left by step with a change of direction. Example 7 - 1 (a) contains a neighboring tone while (b) illustrates a quarter-note passing tone.

Example 7 - 1

The different analysis, of course, results from determining which note is dissonant and therefore nonharmonic.

The lower neighboring tone is common in the style, while its upper counterpart is rare. In example 7 - 2 (a) is a lower neighbor, (b) is consonant and therefore

---

[1]Also often referred to as auxiliaries.

not a true auxiliary, and (c) is a rare upper neighbor.

Example 7 - 2

Where the peak of a figure occurs on an offbeat, as in (b) above, it is customary to follow the high note with a white note value.

While a neighboring note can occur on any off beat, it cannot appear on a beat.

QUARTER NOTE PASSING TONES

A passing tone is a dissonant note approached and left by step in a scalewise motion. When a quarter-note passing tone falls on a beat, it is considered accented. Half-note passing tones and descending quarter-note passing tones can occur on beats two and four. A passing tone never falls on beats one or three, but on any offbeat passing tones may either ascend or descend.

A passage of four descending quarter notes[2] in which the next to last note is an accented passing tone should be followed by a change of direction. Jeppesen calls this figure a "filled out" Nota Cambiata. Note the similiarity between the quarter-note passage at (a) and the Cambiata at (b).

Example 7 - 3

note.[2]A tie or dot may substitute for the first quarter

36

In two-part counterpoint the passing tone should be both preceded and succeeded by consonant intervals. Accented quarter-note passing tones are never followed by eighth notes.

NOTA CAMBIATA

In the Nota Cambiata the first and third notes are consonant, while the second and fourth notes may be dissonant or consonant. When the second note is dissonant, it constitutes the only stylistically acceptable use of the escape tone. The fourth note can be a passing tone if its placement in the measure permits. The first note of the Nota Cambiata must be consonant for its entire duration. In the following, which illustrates various rhythmic treatments of the Cambiata, each dissonant interval is checked.

Example 7 - 4

PORTAMENTO

The portamento figure consists of three notes, the middle note being an anticipation occurring on the last half of a strong beat. The figure may be approached stepwise or by a tie. The second note of the figure is a quarter note on the offbeat approached by downward step. The note is repeated on the following beat and thus becomes an anticipation.

Example 7 - 5

In its consonant form the portamento often occurs with the suspension figure where it shortens the duration of the suspension dissonance. Note that the preparation, suspension, and resolution still require three beats.

Example 7 - 6

The consonant portamento may also be used as a purely melodic device with no suspension involved. In this case all three notes of the figure require consonant treatment.

Example 7 - 7

The dissonant portamento places a dissonant anticipation between two consonances. Like in the consonant form, the anticipation can occur only on the last half of beats one or three.

Example 7 - 8

EIGHTH NOTES

Appearing as they do on the last half of a beat in pairs, eighth notes can only be consonances, passing tones, or neighboring tones. They are commonly com-

bined with the portamento to ornament the resolution
of a suspension. Various uses are illustrated by the
following:

    (a)   eighth notes as consonances
    (b)   the first eighth note as a passing tone
    (c)   the second eighth note as a passing tone
    (d)   the first eighth note as a lower neighbor
    (e)   the second eighth note as a lower neighbor
    (f)   the second eighth note as a lower neighbor
          to a portamento
    (g)   the same requiring a sharp to avoid an aug-
          mented second

Example 7 - 9

Notice that the eighth notes are usually approached
from above. Eighth notes as upper neighboring tones
are rare.

SUSPENSIONS

    The suspension device can become monotonous unless
it undergoes variation. Especially in a chain of suspensions, ornamentation is desirable. The portamento
resolution and the portamento with lower neighbor have
been illustrated. Sometimes the portamento figure is
continued for one beat in which case it is followed by
an ascending skip of a third which may or may not be
filled in by an eighth note.

Example 7 - 10

Other variations of the portamento resolution are possible and can be discovered by a study of Palestrina scores.

The change of bass is one remaining means of varying the suspension. It is used both with and without other variations. Whereas the bass of a 7-6, 4-3, or 9-8 suspension does not normally change until the suspension has resolved, it is possible at the time of resolution for the bass to move to some other note consonant with the resolution. Here the change of bass is illustrated in combination with the portamento.

Example 7 - 11

Example 7 - 12 (a) shows a suspension with change of bass, (b) uses the portamento resolution, and (c) illustrates the portamento combined with a lower neighbor.

Example 7 - 12

SUMMARY

Consonances are acceptable on any beat or fraction of a beat. The following summarizes the appropriate placement of nonharmonic tones.[1]

1	-	2	-	3	-	4	-
S	N	♩ PT	N	S	N	♩ PT	N
	♪↑↓ PT	♪↓ PT	♪↑↓ PT		♪↑↓ PT	♪↓ PT	♪↑↓ PT
	E		E		E		E
	P				P		

---

[1] S = suspension

♩ PT = half-note tone

♪↓ PT = black-note passing tone, descending

♪↑↓ PT = black-note passing tone, ascending or descending

N = neighboring tone (usually lower)

E = escape tone of the Nota Cambiata

P = portamento

Eighth notes occuring on the last quarter of a beat are consonances, passing tones, or neighboring tones.

ASSIGNMENTS:

1. Analyze each black note in <u>Sancti mei</u> by Lassus.[2]
   Keep a frequency tally for each type of nonharmonic tone.
2. Write phrases in two parts using quarter notes as passing tones and neighboring tones.
3. Set the Nota Cambiata in these ways:
   a) all notes consonant
   b) second note dissonant
   c) second and fourth notes dissonant
4. Write a fragment to illustrate each:
   a) a portamento resolution of the suspension
   b) a consonant portamento not associated with a suspension
   c) a dissonant portamento
5. Write a phrase using eighth notes to create the following:
   a) a passing tone
   b) a neighboring tone
   c) an ornamented suspension
6. Write a phrase which will involve three different treatments of the suspension.
7. Add a counterpoint above this <u>cantus firmus</u>.

8. Use all note values in a phrase involving imitation.
9. Set these texts using all note values and imitation:
   a) In your patience possess ye your souls.
   b) He that loveth his life shall lose it.
   c) Crucifixus etiam pro nobis.
   d) A text of your choosing.

[2]See Appendix, pp. 121-122.

CHAPTER EIGHT: JOINING PHRASES

An examination of sixteenth-century compositions reveals that, regardless of the number of voice lines, the structure was typically through-composed with each new phrase starting a fresh point of imitation. Phrases generally overlapped so that the sound was continuous from beginning to close with care being taken to provide adequate rests for breathing. The rests, which corresponded to the punctuation, might or might not involve actual cadences.

THE HOCKET CADENCE

The term hocket (literally, hiccough), as used by music historians, refers to a practice originating early in the Middle Ages of breaking up a melody by the use of rests. Sometimes a melody was tossed back and forth between two voices in such a manner that notes and rests alternated as in Example 8 - 1.

Example 8 - 1

Such naive treatment did not survive into the Renaissance, but a special use of truncated phrases was popular in the sixteenth century. It was the hocket cadence, employed to achieve musical punctuation without stopping the flow of sound.

In a typical two-part hocket, voice A approaches the cadence with a whole note which is a step above the final cadence point. Voice B approaches by a suspension figure in which the resolution of the suspension creates a half-note leading tone.[1] Voice A interrupts its progress to the cadence point with a rest,

[1]Except in the Phrygian mode where the whole- and half-step relationship is reversed.

while voice B resolves the leading tone to the cadence note. Voice A then begins a new phrase while voice B holds the cadence note. Voice B rests before imitating the phrase just introduced by voice A. Notice in Example 8 - 2 that voice A can be either above or below voice B.

Example 8 - 2

NON-CADENTIAL PUNCTUATION

A study of the compositions in the Appendix reveals that phrases often overlap in such a manner that the listener detects no cadence. In the Agnus Dei by Josquin des Prez[2] the upper voice consists of ten phrases of greatly varying length, while the lower voice comprises nine. The rests occur at punctuation of the text, though some punctuation also takes place within a phrase. Note that at no point are both voices resting simultaneously. There are cadences of varying strengths, but none employ the hocket in the form that became a cliché in the sixteenth century.

In Beatus vir by Lassus[3] a hocket on meditabitur divides the composition into almost equal halves. His

---

[2] See Appendix, pp. 123-124.

[3] See Appendix, pp. 117-118.

Oculus non vidit[4] is divided into three parts by strong cadences in measures 9 and 20, the second of which is a hocket. His Sancti mei[5] has principal cadences in measures 12, 17, and 27, with the first and third employing the hocket device.

There was considerable diversity of cadential treatment. It should also be noted that while interior cadences occurred on a variety of pitches within a composition, the note B was excluded as a cadence point.[6]

Repetition and restatement were rare, as form was not a major concern of Renaissance composers. Two distinguishing features of the style did, however, tend to give shape to a composition. Suspensions were used to call attention to major cadences, and each interior cadence was generally followed by a new point of imitation.

ASSIGNMENTS:

1. Sing examples of two-part counterpoint noting the relation of cadences to text punctuation.
2. Write a three-phrase composition. Connect the phrases by means of the hocket and follow each cadence with a fresh point of imitation.
3. Set the following text using non-cadential punctuation (rests) at the commas and a hocket at the semicolon: Go to the ant, thou sluggard; consider her ways, and be wise.
4. Select a text with punctuation of varying strengths. Set it, choosing appropriate cadential treatment.

[4]See Appendix, pp. 119-120.

[5]See Appendix, pp. 121-122.

[6]According to G. F. Soderlund (Direct Approach to Counterpoint), the common cadence points for each mode were:

Dorian	DAF	Mixolydian	GDC
Phrygian	EAG	Aeolian	ADC
Lydian	FAC	Ionian	CGA

5. Take the English translation of a Lassus composition[7], and set it using cadence treatment similar to the original.

[7]See Appendix, pp. 118, 120, 122.

CHAPTER NINE: INVERTIBLE COUNTERPOINT

It is sometimes desirable to use the same material two times with an interchange of voices. The material may involve imitation, canon, or completely different lines. While invertible counterpoint[1] was not as extensively practiced in the sixteenth century as in later periods, the aspiring contrapuntalist will accept the challenge of operating within the confines of the Palestrina style.

In invertible counterpoint a line which was above another becomes the lower in a restatement. There may be a simple exchange of parts or there may be a rearrangement involving other voices.

```
S  ////////         0000000
A     0000000----------
T            xxxxxx////////
     (a)             (b)
```

When an exchange of voices finds a melodic line moving an octave while another line is repeated at its original level, the counterpoint is said to be invertible at the octave. Other intervals of inversion are the double octave (fifteenth), the twelfth, and, less commonly, the tenth.

If the first interval, sounded when the alto enters at (a) above, is a third, the corresponding point at (b) would have an interval of a sixth if line //////// dropped an octave and line 0000000 remained at its original level. Had line //////// dropped a twelfth, the corresponding interval would have been a tenth. Note from the following table that the sum of an interval and its inversion is always one more than the interval of inversion.

[1]Also called "double counterpoint."

TABLE OF INVERSIONS

OCTAVE	Interval	1	2	3	4	5	6	7	8		
	Inversion	8	7	6	5	4	3	2	1		
FIFTEENTH	Interval	1	2	3	4	5	6	7	8	9	10
	Inversion	15	14	13	12	11	10	9	8	7	6
"	Interval	11	12	13	14	15					
	Inversion	5	4	3	2	1					
TWELFTH	Interval	1	2	3	4	5	6	7	8	9	10
	Inversion	12	11	10	9	8	7	6	5	4	3
"	Interval	11	12								
	Inversion	2	1								
TENTH	Interval	1	2	3	4	5	6	7	8	9	10
	Inversion	10	9	8	7	6	5	4	3	2	1

When writing in more than two voices, it is possible to move a line up or down an interval equal to the interval of inversion. For instance, in a four-voice work the bass line might move up to the soprano. However, in two-part writing restrictions of range make it more practical to adjust both voices so that when the voices switch lines a transposition takes place. When this occurs the interval of inversion can be found by selecting an interval, adding the corresponding interval in the inversion and subtracting one. Also, the sum of the transpositions will be one more than the interval of inversion.

In Example 9 - 1a line B is moved up an octave, while line A remains at the original pitch. Since after the exchange the tenor is uncomfortably high, a transposition is recommended to bring the lines into a suitable range. In Example 9 - 1b line A is transposed down a sixth and line B is transposed up a third at the time of exchange of voices. It is often necessary to stop the imitation before the final cadence in order to end in the starting mode.

Example 9 - 1a

Example 9 - 1b   Transposed Version

COUNTERPOINT INVERTIBLE AT THE OCTAVE

Inversion at the interval of the octave is common since it presents few problems. It is sufficient that the student remember that a fifth, which is consonant, inverts to a fourth, which is dissonant, and that the octave inverts to a unison which has restrictions upon its placement. Useful suspensions are the 7-6 and the 2-3 which invert to each other. The 4-3 suspension which inverts to 5-6 may now also be used.

In Example 9 - 2 (a) is correct while the inversion at (b) misuses the intervals of the unison and the fourth.

Example 9 - 2

COUNTERPOINT INVERTIBLE AT THE FIFTEENTH

The treatment of the fifth (twelfth) is the same as in counterpoint invertible at the octave. The fifth (twelfth) may be used only as a passing tone or in a 5-6 (12-13) which will become a 4-3 suspension in inversion.

Often the voices involved in inversion at the fifteenth are not adjacent. In two-part counterpoint there should be a judicious mixture of simple and compound intervals. In Example 9 - 3 each line moves one octave rather than one line moving two octaves with the other repeating at the original pitch. The phrases are joined by a hocket and the first cadence is free.

Example 9 - 3

COUNTERPOINT INVERTIBLE AT THE TWELFTH

This type of inversion is also very useful. A 2-3 suspension becomes a 4-3 and vice versa. The 7-6 suspension can be used only if the sixth continues downward by step, since in the inversion the sixth will become a seventh which will have to be treated as a passing tone. Parallel sixths cannot be used as they invert to sevenths.

Note that A in Example 9 - 4 moves down a sixth while B moves up a seventh.

Example 9 - 4

COUNTERPOINT INVERTIBLE AT THE TENTH

This type of inversion is infrequent because it is the most difficult to handle. Parallel tenths become parallel unisons, parallel thirds become parallel octaves, and parallel sixths become parallel fifths. Consequently, no parallel intervals are possible. Also, thirds and sixths must be approached with care because of the rules governing the approach to the octave and fifth. The only possible suspension is the 2-3 which becomes 9-8, a suspension rarely used in two parts.

In Example 9 - 5 the upper voice is duplicated a tenth below. The three staves are not intended to be performed together. The student may want to approach invertible counterpoint (at any interval) by this method which makes the consequences of inversion immediately apparent.

It is necessary to stop the imitation to achieve a satisfactory cadence. When the voices cross (as in the third measure) the table of inversion no longer applies.

To be useful in a two-part composition, some transposition would be necessary to place the two pairs of voices in the same range. If A were to move down a fifth, B would move up a sixth. Any moves totalling eleven (one more than the interval of inversion) would be possible.

Example 9 - 5

Palestrina rarely continued invertible counterpoint very far into the phrase. However, the student should sustain the inversion as long as is practical in his exercises. It is even possible to combine invertible counterpoint with devices such as augmentation, diminution, and mirroring. Such mental gymnastics appealed to some contrapuntalists of the sixteenth century.

ASSIGNMENTS:

1. Write a phrase of nonimitative invertible counterpoint on three staves to illustrate each:
   a) At the octave
   b) At the twelfth
   c) At the fifteenth
   c) At the tenth
2. Turn each of the above into a two-phrase composition by means of transposition and a hocket. Some
   freedom may be necessary at the cadences.
3. Write a two-phrase setting involving imitative
   invertible counterpoint for each:
   a) At the octave--The fool hath said in his heart,
                     There is no God.
   b) At the twelfth--The law of the Lord is perfect,
                      converting the soul.
   c) At the fifteenth--Laudamus te. Benedicimus te.

CHAPTER TEN:
COUNTERPOINT IN THREE PARTS--CONSONANCES; CADENCES

As mentioned in previous chapters, the basic dif-
ference between counterpoint of the Renaissance and
that of the Baroque era was that the former was linear
in conception while the latter was chord dominated.
While Renaissance composers were not oblivious to the
aggregate sound, their main concern was that each voice
line agree with the lowest part. The resulting chords
were the by-product of the movement of melodic lines.

SONORITIES

Three-part sonorities employing only consonances
above the bass are the triad in root position ($^5_3$), the
triad in first inversion ($^6_3$), and the six-five chord.
The latter, due to the second between the upper parts,
requires special handling and will be treated in a
later chapter.

Example. 10 - 1

These structures can be built upon any white note except B as well as upon B-flat.[1]

Major and minor triads appear in root position or
first inversion. The second inversion ($^6_4$) is considered dissonant because of the fourth above the bass
which must be resolved. Diminished and augmented
triads appear only in first inversion. The diminished
triad is found most often at cadences while the augmented triad lends poignancy to certain words.[2]

Accidentals allowable are the same as in two-part
writing. In addition to the raised leading tone and
the corrected tritone, the style demands that if the
third is present in the final chord of a composition
that it be major. Thus a composition in the Phrygian
mode would end with an E major triad.[3]

[1]The first inversion is available on B since there
is no diminished fifth.

[2]Such as death, tears, grief, etc.

[3]No chord may contain more than one accidental.

While full triad sonority is desirable, it is also possible to double any chord member. A note can even be tripled at the beginning or close of a phrase. Sonorities in which a tone is doubled are illustrated:

Example 10 - 2

Close spacing is preferable, but a spread of more than an octave can be effective between the two lower voices if not maintained for too long a time. The governing factor is the contour of the individual melodic line.

FINAL CADENCES

Concluding cadences may now be of three types: authentic, Phrygian, and plagal. Of these, the first two add a voice to the clausula vera which was standard in two-part writing.

In the authentic cadence the upper voices approach the final note in a stepwise manner, while the lowest voice leaps up a fourth or down a fifth. The result will be recognized as the V to I cadence of functional harmony. Of the two cadence chords, the first is complete while the second is incomplete. If the clausula vera resolves normally, the phrase ends with a triple final, but stepwise movement in parallel thirds is possible to produce a double final and a third. Note that by the addition of a third part, the 7-6 and 2-3 suspensions both become 4-3 suspensions.

Example 10 - 3

The Phrygian cadence uses a stepwise approach to the final in the outer voices. An inner third voice creates a complete minor chord in first inversion which progresses to a major chord with doubled final and with the fifth omitted. In functional harmony it would be analyzed as IV to V, based on the harmonic minor scale.[4]

Example 10 - 4

The Phrygian cadence is available on E or, with a B-flat, on A. It is the only cadence where the final is approached by a half step from above and a whole step from below.

The plagal cadence involves two chords in root position with the root of the first a fourth above or a fifth below the root of the second. If the first triad is complete, the second will have the third omitted as in (a). If the first has no fifth, the final chord will be complete as in (b).

Example 10 - 5

[4] Bach had problems harmonizing chorales in the Phrygian mode. In spite of heroic efforts to make the final cadence sound convincing, he was not always successful. See chorales #3, 10, 16, 21, and 34.

The following concluding cadences are available:

```
On A        Authentic, plagal, Phrygian
   B        None
   B-flat   Authentic, plagal (transposed mode)
   C           "          "
   D           "          "
   E        Phrygian,     "
   F        Authentic,    "
   G           "          "
```

INTERIOR CADENCES

Each type of cadence suitable to end a composition is also available as an interior cadence. However, Renaissance usage avoids disrupting the flow by several means.

It is possible to stagger the phrase endings so that punctuation of individual lines is achieved without any cadential implication. The following example by Palestrina is typical.

Example 10 - 6

The authentic cadence is frequently given a hocket treatment. In a three-part hocket the two upper voices resolve the clausula vera by stepwise motion to the final. The lowest voice, which forms the root of the V chord, replaces the expected skip to the final by a rest. After the resting lowest voice resumes, the other voices are free to drop out, though they usually do not begin to rest simultaneously.

Example 10 - 7

The leading tone cadence is used only for interior phrases. It is of the <u>clausula vera</u> variety and consists of a complete diminished triad in first inversion which progresses to a double final plus a fifth or a third.

Example 10 - 8

The deceptive cadence is an interrupted authentic cadence in which the V chord is followed by VI, IV in first inversion, or, occasionally, by IV in root position. The following example by Victoria illustrates V to VI. Note that the lower voices do not cadence.

Example 10 - 9

The rule about ending with a major triad applies only to final cadences. Interior phrases may end with either a major or minor chord. Any phrase may end with an incomplete chord or a tripled final.

HARMONIC MOVEMENT

Phrases typically begin with a point of imitation, though it is possible for all voices to commence together.

Repeated notes should be used sparingly.

Parallel fifths and octaves are not used, but hidden fifths and octaves are permissible if one part moves by step. The upper voice may skip downward only.

Example 10 - 10

Unisons may now occur between any two parts on any beat if approached by contrary or oblique motion. The only note which cannot be doubled is the leading tone (in a cadence). A unison plus an octave can only be used to begin or close a phrase.

When three parts move in similar motion, not more than two of them may skip.

Except at cadences, functional harmony was not a concern of composers during the Renaissance. Root movement by fourths and fifths was favored, though it did not dominate.[5] Root movement by seconds was prevalent, and movement by thirds was fairly common. The student need not be too concerned with root movement. Functional symbols used in this chapter to clarify the cadences have little meaning for modal counterpoint.

In exercises involving three or more parts, the student should check each pair of voices making sure that the lowest voice makes correct counterpoint with each of the other voices. The rule concerning the unison is relaxed as previously noted. Pairs of voices not involving the bass may contain fourths (singly or in succession), but otherwise should make acceptable counterpoint.

[5]Baroque concepts of tonality and modulation to related keys was predicated on root movement by fourths and fifths.

60

Assignments should now be written on three staves to encourage independent lines. For the present it is advisable to identify each interval, counting from the lowest voice.

ASSIGNMENTS:

1. Analyze all the cadences in the Credo on pp. 125-127 of the Appendix.

2. Write short phrases using only consonances and ending with these final cadences:
   a) authentic
   b) plagal
   c) Phrygian

3. Write two phrases joined by:
   a) non-cadential staggered treatment
   b) A hocket cadence
   c) a leading-tone cadence
   d) a deceptive cadence

4. Using points of imitation, make a three-part setting of these texts:
   a) Hear the right, O Lord; attend unto my cry.
   b) All things come of Thee, and of Thine own have we given Thee.
   c) Patrem omnipotentum, factorum coeli et terrae.
   d) Any text of your choosing.

CHAPTER ELEVEN:
THREE-PART TREATMENT OF NONHARMONIC TONES

The nonharmonic tones allowed in three-part writing are the same as those presented previously. As each nonharmonic tone is reviewed, observations will be made pertinent to its use in three parts.

PASSING TONES

Half note passing tones can occur ascending or descending on beats two and four against a holding note in another part. A third voice may also move in similar values so long as it is consonant with the passing tone. Thus, two moving voices may constitute double passing tones in parallel motion (a), double passing tones in contrary motion (b), a passing tone against consonant stepwise motion (c), or a passing tone against a harmony skip that is consonant with both the passing tone and the holding note (d).

Example 11 - 1

The holding voice can be in any part so long as the upper voices agree with the bass.

Example 11 - 2

It will be remembered that quarter-note passing tones are allowed on all offbeats ascending or descending. Passing tones are not allowed on beats one and three, and they are permitted on beats two and four in a descending line only. Where a passage of four or more quarter notes involves an accented passing tone, the passage must change direction by step following the resolution of the passing tone.

Example 11 - 3

It is possible that in a black-note passage an unaccented passing tone may be followed by an accented passing tone. Here again there must be a change of direction on the next beat.

Example 11 - 4

Where two parts are moving in unequal values it is not necessary that they be consonant with each other. In Example 11 - 5, by Palestrina, the upper voice creates parallel fourths with the bass by following an unaccent passing tone with an accented one, and, at the same time, creates parallel seconds with the middle voice.

Example 11 - 5

Quarter-note passing tones can occur in any voice. When they appear in the lowest part, one of the other voices assumes the role of stabilizer. In the following example the bass contains three passing tones as figured against the middle voice, but only one as figured from the highest voice.

Example 11 - 6

Eighth notes, occurring as they do on the second half of the beat, will be consonant or involve either passing tones or neighboring tones.

SUSPENSIONS

The following suspensions are possible in three parts: 7-6, 2-3, 4-3, and 9-8 (or 2-1). While most cadences involve suspensions, the device may also occur within the phrase. As in two-part writing, suspensions fall only on beats one and three, and may or may not be ornamented.

The 7-6 Suspension

The 7-6 suspension results in a first inversion at the point of resolution. At the point of suspension the third voice may form a third, a fifth, or an octave with the lowest voice. The note of resolution (the sixth) should not be present at the point of suspension.[1]

If the fifth is present with the suspension, it should resolve stepwise upward (a) or move down a

---

[1]It should be observed that, in general, the note of resolution is not present with the suspension dissonance except in the case of the 9-8 (2-1) suspension. While in multi-voiced compositions exceptions may be encountered, the rule holds for thee-part writing.

65

third (b) to avoid a dissonance with the note of resolution.

Example 11 - 7

The 7-6 suspension is often associated with the leading tone and Phrygian cadences. Cadence (a) above would not be possible on D or A because of the doubled leading tone. The figuring $\frac{7}{3}$ would make a more satisfactory cadence.

The 2-3 Suspension

In the 2-3 suspension the added interval is usually the fourth, the fifth, or the sixth, though occasionally a third is used. The added note may remain if it is consonant with the resolution, though it may move to another consonance. The sixth above the suspended note must move to avoid forming a dissonance with the note of resolution.

Example 11 - 8

In (d) above each of the upper voices agrees with the bass, but the b in the top voice has the effect of a passing tone on the wrong beat because of the clash with the inner voice.

It should be noted that the fourth in example (a) is treated as a consonance (not resolved). This treatment of the fourth in connection with the 2-3 suspension is allowed.

The 4-3 Suspension

The most frequent suspension in three-part writing is the 4-3 variety. As was observed in the previous chapter, both the 7-6 and 2-3 suspensions, by the addition of a third voice below, turn into 4-3 suspensions.

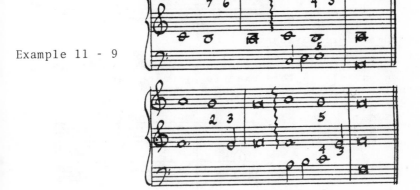

Example 11 - 9

In Example 11 - 9 a fifth above the bass is present with each 4-3 suspension. The added voice may also be a sixth above the bass which may remain or move downward at the time of resolution as in (b). The latter treatment results in the progressions I$_4^6$ to V which has strong cadential implications.

Example 11 - 10

If the added voice is an octave above the bass it may remain. The b in Example 11 - 11 need not be flatted to correct the tritone, as a fourth, either perfect or augmented, is considered a dissonance to be resolved.

Example 11 - 11

The 9-8 (2-1) Suspension

The 9-8 and 2-1 suspensions are used sparingly in three parts. In this example by Palestrina a 2-1 suspension is followed by a 4-3 suspension.

Example 11 - 12

A string of suspensions is more typical of the Baroque period than of the sixteenth century. The following Palestrina example is notable in its consecutive use of 4-3, 9-8, and 7-6 suspensions followed by a $\frac{6}{5}$ chord which receives suspension-type resolution. (The $\frac{6}{5}$ chord will be treated in the following chapter.)

Example 11 - 13

Change of Bass

In all suspensions other than the 2-3 (which is in the lowest voice) a change of bass is possible. When this occurs the bass moves (as the suspension resolves) to another note consonant with the resolution. In the case of the 7-6 suspension, the change of bass may result in a triad in root position.

Example 11 - 14

If the bass moves down a third and the added voice moves up stepwise, a first inversion will result, but the triad will not be the same as that resulting from the normal resolution. Compare (a) and (b).

Example 11 - 15

Sometimes an upward leap in the bass will result in a crossing of parts.

Example 11 - 16

Double Suspensions

The 7-6 and 4-3 suspensions may be combined, as may the 9-8 and 4-3 suspensions. Though double suspensions are possible in three-part writing, they are more typical of four-part counterpoint. Often the rhythmic treatment of the two suspensions is different. If a 4-3 suspension is placed above a 7-6 suspension, the resulting parallel fifths can be corrected by the use of a portamento resolution of one of the suspensions.

Example 11 - 17

NEIGHBORING TONES

Neighboring tones will present no problem if the student bears in mind that auxiliaries are only permissible on offbeats, that two parts moving together in equal values should be consonant with each other, and that each upper voice should agree with the bass. Double lower neighboring tones moving in parallel thirds are possible as quarter notes or eighth notes. The following example illustrates:
- a) a passing tone moving consonantly with a lower neighbor
- b) unequal values producing parallel seconds
- c) double neighboring tones
- d) an ornamental resolution of the 7-6 suspension

Example 11 - 18

THE NOTA CAMBIATA

As in two-part writing, the first and third notes
of the Nota Cambiata should be consonant for their
entire duration when figured from the lowest voice.
What transpires in the other voices is not crucial.
In this six-part example by Palestrina two simultaneous
Nota Cambiatas in different rhythms agree with the bass
while dissonant elements in the form of a passing tone
and a 4-3 suspension occur in the top voice.   In both
Nota Cambiatas the second note is an escape tone.

Example 11 - 19

PORTAMENTO

The portamento, whether used as an ornamental resolution of a suspension or independently as a melodic
figure, tends to agree with other moving parts.   In
Example 11 - 19 the portamento in the highest voice
moves in parallel sixths with the lower Nota Cambiata.

Three treatments of the portamento figure are
illustrated in Example 11 - 20:
   (a)   consonant portamento--ornamental resolution
   (b)   double consonant portamento--independent
         melodic figures
   (c)   double dissonant portamento

Example 11 - 20

Note that in all three of the above the rhythmic treatment of the moving parts differs.

ASSIGNMENTS:

1. Illustrate the following passing tones:
   a) Double half-note passing tones in contrary motion
   b) An unaccented passing tone followed by an accented passing tone
   c) Passing tones illustrating parallel sevenths between the upper two voices
   d) Eighth-note passing tones
2. Illustrate the following suspensions:
   a) A 7-6 suspension used in a phrase which ends with an authentic cadence involving a 4-3 suspension
   b) A 2-3 suspension in a phrase which ends with a Phrygian cadence prepared by a 7-6 suspension
   c) 7-6 and 9-8 suspensions becoming 7-3 and 9-5 through change of bass
   d) A double suspension in which one suspension is ornamented
3. Illustrate these remaining nonharmonic devices:
   a) A lower neighboring tone moving consonantly with a quarter-note passing tone
   b) Double neighboring tones
   c) The Nota Cambiata
   d) A consonant portamento
   e) A dissonant portamento
4. Set these phrases using an assortment of nonharmonic tones:
   a) Hosanna in excelsis
   b) Et in Spiritum sanctum
   c) Heaven and earth are full of thy glory
   d) He was wounded for our transgressions

THE REGULAR SIX-FIVE CHORD

Although the basic sonority employed in modal counterpoint is the triad in root position or first inversion, one other combination of consonances is possible. The $^6_5$ chord resulting from a perfect fifth and a major or minor sixth above a given bass note, though technically a consonance, is usually treated as a suspension because of the second between the upper voices. In its regular form, it falls on beats one or three. The fifth is prepared on the preceding beat[1] and resolved downward by step while the sixth remains. At the time the dissonance resolves, the bass rises to form a triad in root position.

Example 12 - 1

In Example 12 - 1 (a) the fifth is below the sixth. In (b) the intervals are reversed.

If Roman numerals are assigned it becomes clear that the resolution of the regular $^6_5$ chord involves root movement by fifths. In the above example (a) can be analyzed as VI to II, while (b) is II to V. In both instances a seventh chord in first inversion resolves to a triad in root position.

The $^6_5$ in which the fifth is diminished occurs only rarely. The V^7 sound resulting from a diminished fifth and a minor sixth is foreign to the style and should be avoided.

[1] If one considers that the upper voices constitute a 2-3 or 7-6 suspension, the treatment becomes clear.

Example 12 - 2

THE SIX-FIVE WITH THE SIXTH PREPARED

Sometimes the sixth is prepared and the fifth enters freely on a strong beat. In that case the sixth joins the fifth on the following weak beat.

Example 12 - 3

While this treatment of the $\frac{6}{5}$ chord is considerably less effective than the regular treatment, there are times when this solution is useful.

FREE TREATMENT OF THE SIX-FIVE

A $\frac{6}{5}$ chord may occur on a weak beat or offbeat as a result of voices moving in different values. When this occurs, it is sufficient that each voice agree with the bass.

Example 12 - 4

In (a) above the sixth is prepared and the fifth

produces an accented passing tone against it while agreeing with the bass. In (b) the sixth and fifth enter simultaneously. The fifth produces an accented passing tone against the sixth.

THE CONSONANT FOURTH

In two-part writing the fourth was always considered a dissonance. In three or more parts a fourth on a weak beat approached stepwise may constitute the preparation of a 4-3 suspension under certain conditions. It is necessary that the bass be sustained for at least four beats extending from the beat before the consonant fourth through the resolution of the suspension. It is also necessary for the fifth above the bass to enter by step or leap at the point of suspension.

Example 12 - 5

THE SIX-FIVE CHORD COMBINED WITH THE CONSONANT FOURTH

A favored cadence formula is one which combines the two devices studied in this chapter. The regular $\frac{6}{5}$ chord is treated in the normal manner except that the bass does not ascend when the dissonance between the upper parts resolves. The result is a triad in second inversion. The fourth above the bass then becomes the preparation of a suspension.

In this excerpt from Palestrina the middle voice prepares the fifth of the $\frac{6}{5}$ chord which then is given a portamento resolution. The resolution becomes the preparation of a 4-3 suspension.

75

Example 12 - 6

ASSIGNMENTS:

1. Write short excerpts illustrating:
   a) a regular $\frac{6}{5}$
   b) a $\frac{6}{5}$ with sixth prepared
   c) free treatment of the $\frac{6}{5}$

2. Illustrate:
   a) a consonant fourth
   b) a $\frac{6}{5}$ chord combined with a consonant fourth

3. Set each phrase using a $\frac{6}{5}$ on the underlined syllable and a consonant fourth approaching the cadence:
   a) My heart cr<u>i</u>eth out to Thee, O Lord.
   b) They have t<u>a</u>ken a<u>way</u> my Lord.
   c) He filleth the h<u>un</u>gry with good things.

The musical Renaissance is generally considered to have begun around 1450 when a bass voice was added to the typical three voices of the late Middle Ages. Throughout the Renaissance, vocal polyphony normally employed at least four voices, though, as a result of extended rests and delayed entries, the texture actually included much two- and three-part writing. The movements of two representative Palestrina Masses employ the following number of voices:

	L'Homme armé	Ut Re Mi Fa Sol La
Kyrie	5	6
Gloria	5	6
Credo	5 (Crucifixus 4)	6 (Crucifixus 4)
Sanctus	5	6 (Pleni sunt coeli 4)
Hosanna	5	6
Benedictus	4	4
Agnus Dei I	5	6
Agnus Dei II	6	7

The Crucifixus from Missa L'Homme armé is typical of Palestrina's contrapuntal style.[1] The soprano voice is imitated at the fifth below by the alto voice which enters in the middle of the second measure. In measure 8 the tenor enters with a new statement which is then picked up by the alto and soprano and restated in part by the tenor. Not until measure 16 does the bass entrance create four-part counterpoint. After four measures the texture is reduced to two parts. Shortly a third voice enters and, for brief moments in measures 32 and 35, new entries create four parts. Finally, in measures 38 all four parts are well established, and the texture remains basically four-part till the end of the section.

VOICE LEADING

By comparing the bass of the Crucifixus with each of the other three parts, one can observe that the

[1]See Appendix, pp. 167-168.

bass makes correct two-part counterpoint with each of the other voices. Fortunately, no new rules are necessary to govern additional voices. However, some easing of the rules pertaining to hidden fifths and octaves is possible.

Until now, the approach to a fifth in similar motion has been permissible if the upper part moved by step and the lower by skip. In three and four parts the upper voice may move downward by skip. In more than four parts the skip may be in either direction.

Example 13 - 1

Heretofore, hidden octaves have been avoided, but in four parts they occur regularly at cadences with the upper note moving by step and the lower by skip.

Example 13 - 2

Octaves approached by skip in similar motion in both voices should be avoided in four or five parts. They occur mostly in works for six or more voices.

HARMONIC MATERIALS AND DOUBLING IN FOUR PARTS

Palestrina, while a master of counterpoint, did on occasion write homophonically. As a starting point for the study of four-part writing, one might analyze the following choral passage reduced from the Improperia.

Example 13 - 3

The chord vocabulary consists primarily of major and minor triads in root position, all with doubled root. The two first inversion triads have a doubled fifth. The only nonharmonic material is an embellished 4-3 suspension which occurs at three different pitch levels.

Of interest are the Responses by Palestrina's contemporary, Ingegneri. Each Response consists of a four-part chordal section followed by imitative three-part writing, after which the chordal section is repeated. An analysis of the four-part portion of Tenebrae factae sunt reveals the following harmonic material.[2]

        Triads in root position--58
            Doubled root   50
            Doubled third   5
            Doubled fifth   3

        Triads in first inversion--5
            Doubled root   0
            Doubled third   3
            Doubled fifth   2

[2]See Appendix, pp. 154-155.

Measure 12, quoted in Example 13-4, contains the only second inversion as well as the only $^6_5$ chord. The second inversion uses one of the fourths as a passing tone and the other as a consonant fourth preparing a suspension. The $^6_5$ is a passing chord on a weak beat.

Example 13 - 4

The treatment of the $^6_5$ chord is basically the same as it was in three-part writing.

a)   The fifth may be prepared in the regular manner.

Example 13 - 5

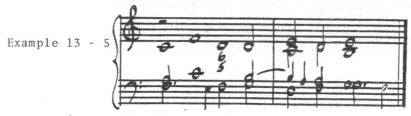

b)   The $^6_5$ may be followed by a consonant fourth, in which case the bass remains.

Example 13 - 6

c)   The sixth may be prepared and then join the fifth, in which case the $^6_5$ is usually followed by a suspension to compensate for the weakness of this treatment. Sometimes a 4-3 suspension occurs simultaneously with the $^6_5$. In Example 13 - 7 Palestrina strengthens the $^6_5$ by both methods.

80

Example 13 - 7

d) On a weak beat or on the last half of any beat, the $^6_4$ may freely result from voice leading (see Example 13 - 4).

DOUBLING IN FIVE PARTS

An analysis of the basically chordal <u>Et in Spiritum sanctum</u> from the Credo of the <u>Missa L'Homme armé</u> yields the following:

Triads in root position--86
3 roots, 1 third, 1 fifth	36
2 roots, 1 third, 2 fifths	29
2 roots, 2 thirds, 1 fifth	11
1 root, 2 thirds, 2 fifths	3
3 roots, 2 thirds	3
4 roots, 1 third	2
1 root, 3 thirds, 1 fifth	1
3 roots, 2 fifths	1

Triads in first inversion--8
1 root, 2 thirds, 2 fifths	3
2 roots, 1 third, 2 fifths	2
1 root, 3 thirds, 1 fifth	2
3 roots, 1 third, 1 fifth	1

Notable are the preponderance of root position chords and the preference for the doubled fifth over the doubled third. There were no second inversions. Only two six-five chords were found, and in both the sixth was treated as a passing tone.

ROOT MOVEMENT

Renaissance root movement is generally thought of as nonfunctional since there is no hierarchy of chords

bearing specific relationships to a tonal center. However, root movement tends to be more functional in some
sixteenth-century works than in others. For example,
the <u>Tenebrae factae sunt</u>, by Ingegneri, has more root
movement by fourths and fifths than does the <u>Crucifixus</u>
from Palestrina's <u>Missa</u> <u>L'Homme armé</u>. But in the chordal <u>Et in Spiritum sanctum</u>, which immediately succeeds
the polyphonic <u>Crucifixus</u>, root movement by fourths and
fifths predominates. The following table compares the
three works:

Root Movement

	Tenebrae	Crucifixus	Et in S.S.
Up a 4th (down a 5th)	16 (22%)	12 (17.6%)	21 (21%)
Down a 4th (up a 5th)	19 (26%)	10 (14.7%)	32 (32%)
Up a 3rd	7 (9%)	9 (13%)	8 (8%)
Down a 3rd	13 (18%)	10 (14.7%)	19 (19%)
Up a 2nd	11 (15%)	19 (28%)	9 (9%)
Down a 2nd	7 (9%)	8 (12%)	10 (10%)
Tritone	1 (1%)		

Total root movement		
By 4ths (5ths)	110	(46%)
By 3rds	66	(27.2%)
By 2nds	65	(26.8%)

The above comparison suggests that texture strongly
influences chord succession. Though Rameau (born in
1683) was the first to define root movement, it is
reasonable to assume that sixteenth-century composers
instinctively concerned themselves to a degree with
root movement in their chordal passages.

Individual styles are also a factor in chord choice.
The <u>Tenebrae factae sunt</u> reveals Ingegneri to be more
influenced than was Palestrina by progressive tendencies
such as accidentals used for color effects and choral
declamation of a text.[3] It is only natural that by the
late sixteenth century some composers would be antici-
pating Baroque functionalism.

It is interesting to compare these limited findings
with the extensive research into root movement in the

[3]Palestrina was not a progressive composer. As
compared with his contemporaries, Palestrina was
reactionary.

Baroque period carried out by A. I. McHose.[4] Both in the Renaissance and in the Baroque period root movement by fourths and fifths predominates. But in the Renaissance root movement by thirds approximates or slightly exceeds movement by seconds, whereas in the Baroque period movement by seconds is more than twice as prevalent as movement by thirds.

CADENCES

Cadences tend toward homophonic texture and functional root movement. In the Crucifixus, four-part cadences at measures 18-19, 48-49, and 60-61 all involve the leading tone. From the reduction in Example 13 - 8 it can be observed that (a) and (c) can be described as VII to I, and (b) as V to I.

Example 13 - 8

The VII to I cadences both employ a 7-6 suspension, while the V to I cadence uses a 4-3 suspension. Comparing the embellished suspensions of (b) and (c) above with cadences of the Improperia (see Example 13-3), one can see that the suspension ornamented with a lower neighbor was a cadential cliché of the style.

In all cadences involving the leading tone, that sensitive pitch is never doubled.

Every cadence used in three-part writing is also available in four or more parts. Example 13 - 9 shows typical treatment of four-part cadences of the following types: (a) authentic, (b) plagal, (c) Phrygian.

[4]Allen Irvine McHose, Basic Principles of the Technique of 18th and 19th Century Composition, p. 129.

83

Example 13 - 9

As in three-part writing, if a third is present in
a concluding cadence, it must be major. Concluding
cadences typically end with a complete triad, though
examples can be found where Palestrina concludes with
a tripled root and a fifth to preserve the clausula
vera treatment of the authentic cadence. A raised
third is never doubled.

Interior cadences include the above, but they may
also be of the leading tone or deceptive types. In
contrapuntal style the voices frequently cadence at
different times. In the concluding measures of the
following Christe eleison, the overall effect suggests
deceptive cadences at (a) and (b), though in actuality
only one or two voices are cadencing. It is the combination of suspension with the raised leading tone
that has cadential implications.

84

Example 13 - 10

NONHARMONIC TONES

Nonharmonic tones present no new problems. As
before, notes moving in similar values should be consonant with each other. Where triple passing tones
move in similar motion, parallel fourths may exist
between two upper parts.

Example 13 - 11

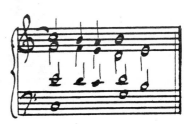

Upper parts moving in dissimilar values need not be consonant with each other.

In single suspensions, the note of resolution should not be present with the suspension, except in the 9-8 suspension. In the next example (a) and (b) are unacceptable, while (c) and (d) are correct.

Example 13 - 12

Double suspensions are fairly common in four or more parts. The usual combinations are $\frac{7-6}{4-3}$ and $\frac{9-8}{4-3}$. In the first of these, parallel fifths will result if the fourth is placed above the seventh. These may be corrected by a portamento resolution of either suspension.

Example 13 - 13

In double suspensions the note of resolution of one suspension may sometimes be present in another part.

Example 13 - 14

86

ASSIGNMENTS:

1. Compare the harmonic materials of three of Palestrina's contemporaries:
   a) Victoria--O vos omnes   Appendix p. 157
   b) Lassus--Penitential Psalm III   Appendix p. 191
   c) Hassler--Quia vidisti me   Appendix p. 158

2. Determine the root movement for the three works in assignment one.

3. Set this text (either English or Latin) chordally in four parts:
   Omnes amici mei dereliquerunt me,
   et praevaluerunt in sidiantes mihi:
   tradidit me quem diligebam.

   All my friends have forsaken me,
   and all my enemies have prevailed against me:
   he whom I loved hath betrayed me.

4. Set this text (either English or Latin) polyphonically in four parts using points of imitation:
   Exaltabo te, Domine, quoniam suscepisti me,
   nec delectasti inimcos meos super me.

   I will exalt Thee, O Lord, for Thou hast upheld me,
   and hast not made mine enemies to rejoice over me.

5. Analyze the harmonic materials in these five-part compositions:
   a) Palestrina--Agnus Dei I from Missa Repleatur os meum laude; Appendix, pp. 179-181
   b) Lassus--Motet: Tristis est anima mea; Appendix, pp. 184-190

6. Set a text of your own choosing in five parts, first chordally and then polyphonically.

CHAPTER FOURTEEN: TRIPLE METER

Meter did not have the same significance in the sixteenth century that it has today. Time signatures used in vocal polyphony did not exercise control over the accentuation of individual lines. Rather, their function was to indicate relationships. The signatures were the remnants of the earlier Mood, Time, and Prolation associated with the fourteenth-century Ars Nova. Those terms correspond to our present division of phrases into measures, measures into beats, and beats into subdivisions.

The following table shows the signatures used in the sixteenth century and their modern equivalents.

Sixteenth century	Modern
☉ Time perfect Prolation perfect	𝄽 Triple compound
O or Φ Time perfect, Prolation imperfect	3/1 (3/2) Triple simple
ℂ Time imperfect Prolation perfect	𝄽 Duple compound
¢ Time imperfect, Prolation imperfect	4/1 Duple simple

Of these, the ☉ was very rare, while the ¢ was by far the most common. Toward the close of the century ℂ was sometimes used for duple simple, especially in secular music, with the quarter note rather than the half note becoming the unit. Thus, ℂ was the equivalent of $\frac{4}{4}$, as it still is today.

Barlines generally did not appear in individual part books, having been reserved for full scores and instrumental works. The rhythmic regularity of much instrumental music of the period was not shared by the vocal style in which agogic accents created an interesting counterpoint of rhythm. Morris transcribes two[1] excerpts from Palestrina's <u>Stabat Mater</u> as follows:[1]

Example 14 - 1

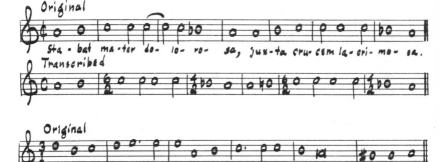

The values are unchanged in the triple meter except to reflect the approximate modern equivalent.

Numbers were used to indicate proportions. Thus, a $\frac{3}{1}$ indicated that a note value moved three times as fast as previously. Either the original signature or an inversion of the proportion $\frac{1}{3}$ restored the original tempo and meter.

The Gloria and Credo movements of a Mass were likely to be interrupted by sections in triple meter. In the Credo of his <u>Missa L'Homme armé</u>, Palestrina employs

[1]R. O. Morris, <u>Contrapuntal Technique in the Six-teenth Century</u>, Musical Examples, p. 6.

triple meter for the phrase <u>Et resurrexit tertia dia</u> and again for the section beginning <u>Et in Spiritum sanctum</u>.[2]

A $\frac{3}{2}$ signature indicates that three beats occupy the time span formerly filled by two. Thus, in <u>Tu pauperum refugium</u>, by Josquin des Prez, the unit becomes one-and-a-half times faster at the first meter change.[3]

Compositions or sections in triple meter in which white notes predominate and in which there are no values shorter than the quarter note are presumed to be in fast triple time. Those employing all values require a moderate pace. An example of the latter is the motet <u>In Festo Apostolorum</u>.[4]

PLACEMENT OF DISSONANCE

The modern meters $\frac{3}{4}$ and $\frac{3}{2}$ (triple simple) are not the musical equivalent of $\frac{6}{8}$ and $\frac{6}{4}$ (duple compound). However, since secondary rhythm was such an important feature of the non-accentual meters of the sixteenth century, we may use $\frac{3}{2}$ and $\frac{6}{2}$ interchangeably in dealing with the slower triple time. Thus, a $\frac{6}{2}$ measure will be treated like a measure and a half of $\frac{4}{2}$. The following could be equally effective in either meter.

Example 14 - 2

[2] See Appendix, pp. 167, 169-170.

[3] See Appendix, p. 156. Proportion is not affected by the reduction of values.

[4] See Appendix, pp. 146-149.

In fast triple time, however, the suspensions would be incorrectly treated in the preceding example, since the preparation, suspension, and resolution would occupy less than three beats. While the suspension dissonance may be encountered on beats one or three, the most common practice was to prepare the suspension on beat one and resolve it on beat three. Thus, the suspension was totally contained within the measure.

Example 14 - 3

There are differing views as to what is normal in Palestrina's treatment of the suspension dissonance in triple time. Morris recognizes only the possibility of placing the suspension on the second beat,[5] whereas Reese says:

> Although stresses may not have been as heavy in this period as later, there would have been no point in confining suspensions, for example, to the first and third beats in binary rhythm or to the first and second beats in ternary rhythm, etc., if there had been no such underlying accentuation.[6]

[5]R. O. Morris, Contrapuntal Technique, p. 39.

[6]Gustave Reese, Music in the Renaissance, p. 461.

According to Soderlund, "The suspension dissonances are found more frequently on beats two and three than on one."[7]

In the light of these divergent views, it would be well to examine a work in triple meter by Palestrina in an attempt to see how he handles the suspension and other nonharmonic devices.[8] In the Hosanna of his O Regem Coeli Mass, three suspensions occur on beat one and eight are found on beat two, while beat three has three single suspensions as well as a double suspension. The work appears to be in fast triple time since white values predominate and there are no values shorter than the quarter note.

In the same Hosanna the Nota Cambiata figure appears seven times. In all but two instances it starts on beat one. The escape tone of the figure is dissonant in three instances and falls on the last half of beat two.

The other nonharmonic material in this work can be summarized thus: one accented descending passing tone (beat two), twenty-one unaccented passing tones (all beats), two lower neighboring tones (on the last half of beat three).

Also notable are the two identical appearances of the $^6_5$ chord in which the fifth is prepared on beat two and the sixth enters by leap on beat three. The fifth resolves downward by step as the bass rises on beat one. Thus, the treatment is regular in all respects except the placement of the dissonance on a weak beat.

The student can be forgiven for some bewilderment at this point concerning what constitutes normal usage in triple meter. He is advised to analyze works in both fast and slow triple meter and draw his own conclusions.

[7]Gustave Soderlund, Direct Approach to Counterpoint, p. 104.

[8]See Appendix, pp. 144-145.

93

ASSIGNMENTS:

1. Locate and identify all nonharmonic tones in the Hosanna found on pp. 144-145 of the Appendix.

2. Analyze the $\frac{3}{1}$ passages in O admirabile commercium and in the Credo of Missa L'Homme armé found in the Appendix on pp. 211-212, 169-170.

3. Analyze the motet In Festo Apostolorum on pp. 146-149 of the Appendix.

4. Set in triple time:

   a) Glory be to God on high
   b) Hosanna in the highest
   c) I await the resurrection of the dead

CHAPTER FIFTEEN: FORM

The Renaissance was a fecund period as composers perfected existing forms and developed new ones in secular and sacred, vocal and instrumental areas. The sixteenth century witnessed the Protestant Reformation which gave rise in different locales to the chorale, the psalter, the anthem, and the Service, all of which began developments that stretched beyond the sixteenth century. The Counter-reformation composers, prodded by the Council of Trent, attempted to bring simplicity, intelligibility, and mysticism to the motet and the Mass, the two forms of Roman church music which reached the pinnacle of their development in the Renaissance.

The scope of this book limits discussion to the sacred vocal form, specifically those employed by Palestrina. His Masses and motets, representing the towering achievement of sixteenth-century sacred polyphony, have for centuries served as the yardstick by which other liturgical music is measured. It is with a survey of the design, techniques, and devices employed in these two forms that we close this study of sixteenth-century polyphony.

THE MASS

The Mass is a liturgical form encompassing the activities of the Eucharist, or Holy Communion. The portions which vary with the calendar or the occasion are called the Proper. A few portions remain constant and are known as the Ordinary. While the entire Mass may be said or chanted, composers have tended to select certain parts of the Ordinary to set polyphonically. Thus, the Mass as a musical form consists normally of the following portions: Kyrie, Gloria, Credo, Sanctus-Benedictus, and Agnus Dei.[1]

Because of its liturgical function, the Sanctus is sometimes split into two movements, the second beginning with the words <u>Benedictus qui venit</u>. In that case the two halves precede and follow the consecration of the bread and wine. The Agnus Dei was also frequently

---

[1]For the English translation of these five portions see Appendix, p. 113-114.

divided into two portions: Agnus Dei I which ended
with <u>Miserere nobis</u>, and Agnus Dei II which closed
with <u>Dona nobis pacem</u>.

In the Missa Brevis homophonic writing predominated, but in more polyphonic settings those movements
having lengthy texts, such as the Credo, were frequently broken up into separate sections. This was especially true of the Masses of later periods intended for the
concert hall.[2] Palestrina typically divided the Credo
into three sections:

<u>Patrem omnipotentem</u>
<u>Crucifixus</u>
<u>Et in Spiritum</u> sanctum

Of these, the texture is reduced in the Crucifixus by
at least one voice part.

Early Masses drew from the stock of Gregorian
chants available for each of the component parts. Later these chants formed the basis of polyphonic treatment of selected portions. While the fourteenth century brought the first polyphonic setting of the entire
Ordinary, unity resulting from common material in all
movements required another century.

METHODS OF CONSTRUCTION

The chant received two types of treatment in the
fifteenth century, one involving a rhapsodic superius
(treble) and the other a slow-moving tenor. In the
Plainsong Mass, also known as the Paraphrase Mass, each
movement borrowed an appropriate Gregorian chant and
ornamented it, usually in the treble. Since each movement originally employed a different chant, the unity
was liturgical rather than musical. Later Plainsong
Masses used one Gregorian melody as a basis for a free
fantasy involving all movements.

In the Cantus Firmus Mass, also known as the Tenor
Mass, one borrowed chant or secular tune unified all
movements. The borrowed melody was originally placed
in the tenor, though in later works it was free to mi-
grate to other parts. The notes of the cantus firmus

[2]As an example, the Credo of Bach's B-minor Mass
divides into seven sections.

generally moved in such long values that the tune was hardly recognizable.

In some Masses the distinction between Paraphrase and Cantus Firmus technique is blurred. Frequently the upper voices anticipate the tenor which is the last to enter. Where considerable imitation is involved, it is not always possible to determine whether the superius or the tenor is the principal voice.

A third method of construction, a favorite with sixteenth-century composers, originated somewhat later. The Parody Mass is based not on a single borrowed melody, but on preexistent secular or sacred polyphony. The adaptation might involve a minimum of reworking, or it might display considerable imagination and ingenuity. Characteristically, the entire polyphonic web of the original appears at some point in the transcription. Compare the opening of the motet <u>Assumpta est Maria</u> with the beginning of the Mass which parodies it.

Example 15 - 1

The second part of the motet finds its echo in the <u>Christe eleison</u> as follows:

Example 15 - 2

Canonic construction, involving strict imitation in each movement of the Mass, is a display of skill. The material may be borrowed or original. An example of canonic construction is <u>Missa repleatur os meum</u>, the first movement of which treats the cantus firmus in the following manner.[3]

Kyrie   Canon at the octave between Tenor and
          Quintus (Soprano II)
          Equivalent of eight whole notes between
          entrances of Leader and Follower
          Alto imitates Soprano I at fifth below
          Bass imitates Tenor at fifth below
          Quintus last to enter

Christus   Canon at the seventh between Tenor and
          Quintus (Soprano II)
          Seven whole notes between entrances of
          of Leader and Follower
          Bass briefly imitates Alto at fifth
          below
          Soprano I briefly imitates Tenor at
          fifth below
          Quintus last to enter

Kyrie   Canon at the sixth between Tenor and
          Quintus (Soprano II)

[3]See Appendix, pp. 172-176.

Six whole notes between entrances of
Leader and Follower
Soprano I imitates Alto at fifth above
Bass imitates Tenor at fifth above
Quintus enters with Bass

Subsequent movements treat the same theme in canons at the fifth, fourth, third, second, and unison. In each the canon occurs between the Tenor and the Quintus, which is usually the last voice to enter. This Quintus does not remain as Soprano II, but becomes Mezzo-Soprano, Alto II, and Tenor II in other movements. Each change of interval between Leader and Follower is accompanied by a shortened time span between entrances so that in Agnus Dei I the canon is at the unison and the time lapse between Leader and Follower is only one whole note.

The Agnus Dei of <u>Missa repleatur os meum</u> is quite remarkable. Agnus Dei I contains Palestrina's only use of an augmentation canon.[4] The first twenty measures of Tenor I expand to forty as Tenor II doubles the note values. To this is added a five-measure codetta with the sustained last note of Tenor II serving as a pedal tone. Palestrina thickens the texture by adding a voice in Agnus Dei II. What is remarkable is that the Quintus and the new Sextus are both in canon with the Tenor, but at different intervals. While the Quintus pursues a canon at the octave, the Sextus engages in a canon at the fourth. The other three voices are involved in rather free imitation.

The cantus firmus, which was derived from a motet by Jacquet of Mantua, undergoes alteration in various movements. The following beginnings illustrate the treatment.

[4]See Appendix, pp. 179-181.

Example 15 - 3

One more method of construction remains which needs little explanation. Where the thematic material is original and there is no extensive use of canon, the construction is said to be free. This does not mean, however, that there are no unifying devices. The Pope Marcellus Mass, though considered free, has one thematic thread running through the various movements.

Example 15 - 4

That melodic thread, with its repeated notes and
ascending leap of a fourth, gives rise to related
themes which in turn provide new motives. The following quotations from Agnus Dei I show how economical
Palestrina was with his material.

Example 15 - 5

A scrutiny of the movement also reveals invertible counterpoint, varied repetition, restatement, and a short coda.[5]

Reese assigns Palestrina's 105 Masses to five categories as follows:[6]

Paraphrase (Plainsong)	35
Tenor (Cantus firmus)	7
Parody	52
Canonic	5
Free	6

Movements of each type of Mass are included in the Appendix.

Paraphrase--De Feria (Kyrie) pp. 139-143
Tenor--L'Homme armé (Kyrie and
  Credo) pp. 162-171
Parody--Assumpta est Maria (Kyrie) pp. 193-196
Canonic--Repleatur os meum
  (Kyrie, Sanctus, and Agnus
  Dei I and II) pp. 172-183
Free--Papae Marcelli (Agnus Dei I) pp. 197-198

It is claimed that approximately four-fifths of Palestrina's Masses draw upon Gregorian chant for thematic material.[7] Without an intimate knowledge of plainsong that few today possess, one can scarcely appreciate the extent and subtlety of Palestrina's borrowing. Even where no borrowing is involved, Palestrina's lines are infused with the spirit of the chant. Compare the opening of the vesper hymn Sanctorum meritas, given in Example 15 - 6, with the tenor of Agnus Dei II from the Mass bearing that title.

[5]See Appendix, pp. 197-198.

[6]G. Reese, Music in the Renaissance, pp. 470-72.

[7]D. Grout, A History of Western Music, 2nd edition, p. 266

Example 15 - 6

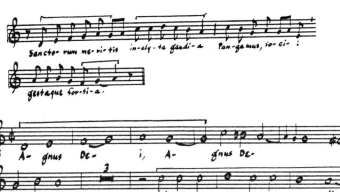

Coates has divided Palestrina's stylistic development into three periods, the first of which was devoted to an exhibition of Palestrina's mastery of the contrapuntal complexities and ingenuities inherited from the Franco-Flemish school.[8] To this period are assigned the cantus firmus Masses and the canonic feats. The second period is thought to have begun with the somewhat austere Pope Marcellus Mass, while the Masses of the last period are supposedly marked by richness and expressiveness representative of Palestrina's highest achievement.

Dates of publication bear little, if any, relationship to dates of composition. The five canonic Masses, for example, were originally published in the following years:

Ad coenam agni providi	1554
Ad fugam	1567
Repleatur os meum	1570
Sacerdotes Domini	1599
Sine nomine	1599

It was not until the nineteenth century that a complete edition of Palestrina's works was undertaken.

[8]H. Coates, Palestrina, p. 105.

REQUIEM MASS

The Requiem Mass is performed in honor of the dead and contains the following musical sections:

Introit	Requiem aeternam
Kyrie	
Gradual and Tract	Requiem aeternam; Absolve Domine
Sequence	Dies Irae
Offertory	Domine Jesu Christi
Sanctus-Benedictus	
Agnus Dei	
Communio	Lux aeterna

Other portions may also be set musically at the discretion of the composer.

It will be noted that of the Ordinary only the Kyrie, Sanctus-Benedictus, and Agnus Dei remain. The more joyful portions have been replaced by items from the Proper. Of these, the most familiar is the Dies Irae which, in the sixteenth century, was usually performed in plainsong in keeping with its great solemnity. The following short melody is repeated for nearly a score of stanzas:

Example 15 - 7

Later composers, attracted by the dramatic possibilities of the Dies Irae text, tended to make it the focal point of the entire work in settings retaining the text but not the plainsong melody.

In the sixteenth century the other portions of the Requiem were generally based upon corresponding plainsong melodies which might receive quite free treatment after the intonation of the opening pitches.

TEXTURE AND MODE

A few comments pertinent to texture and mode are necessary to complete the description of the Mass. The length of a given work was largely determined by its texture. The more polyphonic the treatment, the longer the setting.

Mention has been made of the Missa Brevis in which homophonic writing predominated. This "brief Mass" served three important functions: 1) it enabled small churches not equipped to handle elaborate settings to replace the unadorned chant with part-music; 2) it filled the need for a short service for everyday use even in the larger churches; and 3) it met the demands of the Council of Trent that the words be intelligible and the music unostentatious.

Palestrina, while writing Masses of varying lengths, never approximated the enormity of works of later periods designed for concert use.

Except in the Requiem, one mode prevails for all movements in most sixteenth-century Masses. This results in some tediousness when the musical portions are isolated and performed without the accompanying liturgy of an actual service. Modern listeners tend to become restive, because their ears are accustomed to modulation, a concept which was still rudimentary in Palestrina and his contemporaries.

THE MOTET

The word "motet" has changed its connotation several times during the long history of the form. During the sixteenth century it referred to a short composition based on a sacred Latin text, intended to be sung unaccompanied, and written in a polyphonic or semi-polyphonic style. Like its Anglican counterpart, the anthem, it was intended to be used in a service. While it might be inserted at prescribed places in the Mass, it was primarily associated with the Office of Vespers. Stylistically it is hardly distinguishable from the Mass, but, judging from the vast number of motets written in the Renaissance, composers appreciated the freedom to set texts of their own choosing.

While Lassus is generally acknowledged to be the

supreme master of the motet, both as to quantity and
emotional impact, Palestrina's more than 250 motets
have been called the "purest example of a great epoch."[9]
Reese, in discussing their variety of form, cites the
following types:[10]

```
a B c B
a B c d B e
A b A c A d A e A
A A B B C C D D
A A B B'C C'D D'
a B B'C C'C"D D' E E'
```

The text generates the music, with each phrase
comprising a complete section ending on a cadence
characteristic of the mode. The texture typically
consists of successive points of imitation, though
any section may be chordal or freely polyphonic without involving imitation. A mixture of textures in one
composition is frequent.

The following motets included in the Appendix provide some hint as to the varied approaches to the form:

Four-part
Tu pauperum refugium	Josquin des Pres
O vos omnes	Victoria
Quia vidisti me	Hassler
Veni sponsa Christi	Palestrina
In festo apostolorum:	
Tollite jugum meum	Palestrina
Dies sanctificatus	Palestrina

Five-part
| Tristis est anima mea | Lassus |

Eight-part
| O Admirabile commercium | Palestrina |

Twelve-part
| Laudate Dominum in tympanis | Palestrina |

[9]Grove's Dictionary of Music, 5th edition, Vol. V,
p. 914.

[10]G. Reese, Music in the Renaissance, pp. 462-64.

A discussion of the motet would be incomplete with-
t a mention of text painting. While the madrigalists
ized every opportunity to have the music describe as
terally as possible the meaning of the individual
ˉd, motet writers only occasionally employed musical
ıllustration. The following examples of words inviting
pictorial treatment are typical:

> circumdabit (surround)
> coelo (heaven)
> descendi (descended)

Example 15 - 8

Some suggestions regarding form may prove helpful
to the aspiring contrapuntalist undertaking a complete
work:

(1) Cadences should not be too frequent. Individual voices may cadence while the others flow
on.

(2) The texture in longer works should be varied
by the addition or subtraction of voices and
by a mixture of contrapuntal and homophonic
writing.

(3) In imitative writing the order of entries
should be varied.

(4) All voice lines should be equally interesting
with regard to agogic accents and contour.

(5) A new subject will generally be announced by
a voice that has been resting.

It is not possible to develop a fine sense of style by merely studying the rules. The serious student will involve himself in the music of the period, as both listener and participant. Only thus can the Renaissance be made to live again.

ASSIGNMENTS:

1. Designate by letters the form of the following motets. Use capital letters where both text and music are involved; small letters to refer to the music only.

    Tristis est anima mea   Appendix, pp. 184-190
    Laudate Dominum in tympanis   Appendix, pp. 213-220

2. Analyze the use of canon in Dies Sanctificatus, found on pp. 150-153 of the Appendix.

3. Examine Palestrina's use of this antiphon in his motet, Veni Sponsa Christi, found on pp. 136-138 of the Appendix.

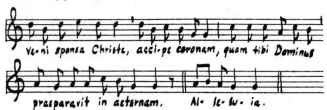

4. Write a motet on a text of your choosing, using a mixture of textures.

A P P E N D I X

CREDITS

Bellingham, B., and E. G. Evans, Jr., eds. Sixteenth-Century Bicinia. Madison, Wisconsin: A - R Editions, 1974.
    Missa Pange Lingua: ·Agnus Dei--Josquin des Prez

Davison, A. T., and Willi Apel, Historical Anthology of Music: Oriental, Medieval, and Renaissance Music, Rev. ed. Cambridge: Harvard University Press, 1949.
    Tu pauperum refugium--Josquin des Prez
    O vos omnes--Victoria
    Quia vidisti me--Hassler
    Penitential Psalm III (excerpts)--Lassus
    Missa Papae Marcelli: Agnus Dei I--Palestrina

Morris, R. O. Contrapuntal Technique in the Sixteenth Century. London: Oxford University Press, 1964.
    Veni Sponsa Christi--Palestrina

Parrish, C., and J. F. Ohl, eds. Masterpieces of Music Before 1750. New York: W. W. Norton, 1951.
    Tristis est anima mea--Lassus

Schmidt-Goerge, J. The History of the Mass. Ed. K. G. Fellerer. Anthology of Music, vol. 30. New York: Broude Brothers.
    Missa Assumpta est Maria: Kyrie--Palestrina

Soderlund, G. F. Examples of Gregorian Chant and Works by Orlandus Lassus, Giovanni Pierluigi Palestrina, and Marc Antonio Ingegneri. 3rd ed. Englewood Cliffs, N.J.: Prentice-Hall, 1947.
    Missa O Regem Coeli: Hosanna--Palestrina
    In Festo Apostolorum: Tollite jugum--Palestrina
    Tenebrae factae sunt--Ingegneri
    O admirabile commercium--Palestrina
    Laudate Dominum in tympanis--Palestrina

Soderlund, G., and S. Scott. Examples of Gregorian
    Chant and Other Sacred Music of the 16th Century.
    Englewood Cliffs, N.J.: Prentice-Hall, 1971.
            Beatus vir--Lassus
            Oculus non vidit--Lassus
            Sancti mei--Lassus
            Missa Jam Christus astra ascenderat: Credo--
                Palestrina
            Magnificat Tertii Toni: Et misericordia--
                Victoria
            Magnificat Secundi Toni: De posuit potentes--
                Victoria
            Missa ad imitationem: Credo--Lassus
            Magnificat (V. 2)--Palestrina
            Missa De Feria: Kyrie--Palestrina
            Dies Sanctificatus--Palestrina
            Missa L'homme armé: Kyrie, Credo--Palestrina
            Missa Repleastur os meum laude: Kyrie,
                Sanctus, Agnus Dei--Palestrina
            Missa Ut Re Mi Fa Sol La: Kyrie, Sanctus--
                Palestrina

TRANSLATION OF THE TEXT OF THE MASS

Kyrie: Lord, have mercy. Christ, have mercy. Lord, have mercy.

Gloria: Glory be to God on high (intoned by the priest).
Choir: And on earth peace to men of good will. We praise thee; we bless thee; We adore thee; we glorify thee. We give thee thanks for thy great glory, O lord, heavenly King. God the Father Almighty. O Lord Jesus Christ, the only-begotten Son: O Lord God, Lamb of God, Song of the Father, who taketh away the sins of the world, have mercy on us: who taketh away the sins of the world, receive our prayers: who sitteth at the right hand of the Father, have mercy on us. For thou only art holy: thou only art Lord: thou only, O Jesus Christ, are most high, together with the Holy Ghost, in the glory of God the Father, Amen.

Credo: I believe in one God (intoned by the priest).
Choir: The Father Almighty, maker of heaven and earth, and of all things visible and invisible. And in one Lord Jesus Christ, the only begotten Son of God, born of the Father before all ages; God of God, light of light, true God of true God; begotten not made; con-substantial with the Father; by whom all things were made. Who for us men, and for our salvation, came down from heaven; and was incarnate by the Holy Ghost, of the Virgin Mary; and was made man. He was crucified also for us, suffered under Pontius Pilate, and was buried. And the third day he rose again according to the scriptures; and ascended into heaven. He sitteth at the right hand of the Father; and he shall come again with glory to judge the living and the dead; and his kingdom shall have no end, and in the Holy Ghost, the Lord and giver of life, who proceedeth from the Father and the Son, who together with the Father and the Son is adored and glorified; who spoke by the prophets. And one holy catholic and apostolic church. I confess one baptism for the remission of sins. And I await the resurrection of the dead, and the life of the world to come. Amen.

Sanctus: Holy, holy, holy, Lord God of hosts. Heaven and earth are full of thy glory. Hosanna in the high-est.
Benedictus: Blessed is he that cometh in the name of the Lord.

Agnus Dei I: Lamb of God, who takest away the sins of the world, have mercy on us.
Agnus Dei II: Lamb of God, who takest away the sins of the world, grant us peace.

I (Dorian)   Alleluia

III (Phrygian)   Kyrie

VII (Mixolydian)   Antiphon

115

116

Cantiones duarum vocum
Beatus vir

Lassus

117

Blessed is the man that shall continue in wisdom, and that shall
meditate in his justice, and in his mind shall think of the all
seeing eye of God.   Eccl. 14:22

Oculus non vidit

Lassus

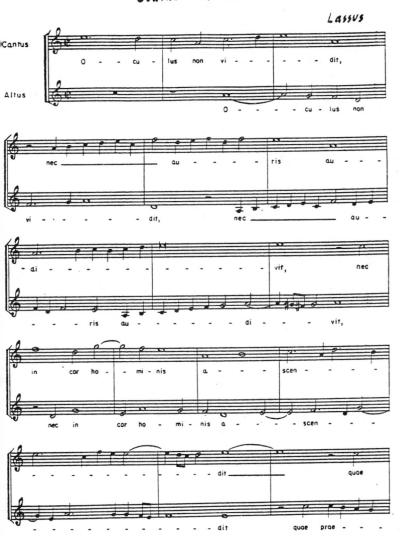

119

That eye hath not seen, nor ear heard, neither hath it entered into
the heart of man, what things God hath prepared for them that love
God.   I Cor. 2:9

Sancti mei

Lassus

My holy people, who in this world have known only toil and strife, I
shall grant to you the reward for all your labors.

Agnus Dei
(Missa Pange Lingua)

[Josquin des Prez]

Missa Jam Christus astra ascenderat: Credo

Palestrina

125

126

127

Magnificat Tertii Toni: Et misericordia

Victoria

129

Magnificat Secundi Toni: Deposuit potentes

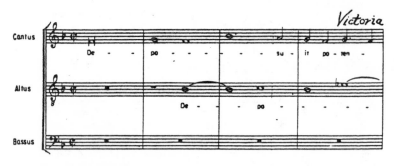

130

Missa ad imitationem moduli Susanne un iour: Credo

Lassus

Magnificat.

And my spirit hath rejoiced in God, my Savior.   Luke 1:47

Reprinted by permission of Oxford University Press

Mass: De Feria: Kyrie.   Palestrina.

MASS: O REGEM COELI : HOSANNA — PALESTRINA

144

MOTET : IN FESTO APOSTOLORUM.

Palestrina

146

Take My yoke upon you, saith the Lord, and
learn of me, because I am meek, and humble of
heart: For My yoke is sweet, and My burden light. Matt. 11:29,30

Motet: Dies Sanctificatus.

Palestrina.

151

The sacred day has dawned upon us, Come ye people and praise God,
Because this day a great light has fallen upon the earth.
(Psalm 117:24): This is the day that the Lord hath made -
let us rejoice and be glad in it.

Response.   Ingegneri.

154

There was darkness over the earth, (Matt. 27:45)
when the Jews had crucified Jesus;
and about the ninth hour Jesus cried out
with a loud voice: My God,
why hast thou forsaken me? (Matt. 27:46)
And bowing his head, he gave up the ghost. (John 19:30)
V. And crying out with a loud voice, he said:
     Father, into thy hands I commend my spirit. (Luke 23:46)
Repeat: And bowing his head....the ghost.

Josquin des Près

Thou art the refuge of the poor, alleviator of weakness, hope of the exiled, strength of the heavy-laden, path for the erring, truth and life. And now, Lord redeemer, I take refuge in thee alone; I worship thee, the true God. In thee I hope, in thee I trust. My salvation, Jesus Christ, uphold me, in order that my soul may never sleep in death.

156

Tomas Luis de Victoria (c. 1540-1611)

O vos omnes

All ye that pass by, behold and see if there be any sorrow
like unto my sorrow.　　Lamentations 1:12

Hans Leo Hassler (1564-1612)

Quia vidisti me

Motet

Because thou hast seen me, Thomas, thou hast believed:
blessed are they that have not seen and yet have believed.
John 20:29

Mass: L'homme armé

Kyrie

Palestrina.

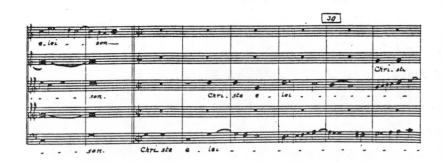

Credo in unum Deum.

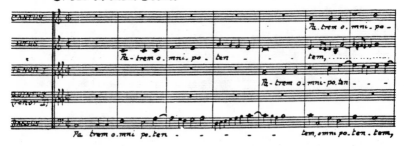

. num Je . sum Chri - stum......... Fi . li um De . i u - ni ge - - ni.
. num Je - sum Chri . stum Fi . li um Dei u - ni ge - - - ni.
.... Je . sum Chri . stum. ....
. . li . - - um. Et ex
Je - sum Chri . stum.
40
. tum. Et ex Patre na . tum an . te o . mni . a sae . - - cu . la.
. tum. Et ex Patre na . tum an . te o . mnia sae . cu . la. ....
Et ex Pa . tre na . - - tum an . te o . mnia sae - cu . la.
Pa . - - . tre na . - - - - - - tum.
Et ex Patre na . tum an . te o . mni a sae - - - cu . la.
50
Deum de De . o, lu men de lu mi . ne, De . um ve . rum de De . o
De . um de De . o lu . men de lu mi . ne, De . um ve . rum...
.... De - um de De . o, ... lumen de lu mi . ne, ... De . um
Lu . - - - - - men de
De . um de De . o lu . men de lumi ne De - um........

60

ve - ro,	de De.o	ve -	-	-	ro,	ge -	ni tum non fa -	-	- ctum
de De.o	ve - ro,	de	De	. o	re .	ro			Con -
ve - rum	de De o	ve -	ro,			ge -	ni tum non fa -	-	ctum
		De -	.	o				ve -	-
ve - rum	de De -	o	ve -	-		ro			con.

70

con. substanti alam	Pa . tri:	per quem o	. mni.a fa	-	cta	sunt.
- . substanti olem	Pa . tri:	per quem omnia	.... facta sunt.	Qui pro .	pter	nos .
		per quem o mni.a fa	- .	cta sunt	Qui propter	nos
-	-	-	ro.			Et
. substanti . a . lem Pa . tri.				Qui	propter nos ho-

Qui propter nos	ho . mi . nes,		et propter nostram salu .	-	-	-
qui propter nos ho . mi . nes		et propter nostram salu tem	da
ho . mi . nes,	et propter nostram salutem, ... nostram salu .	tem	de
pro - . . pter		no - . . -	stram
. . mi . nes, ...	et pro . pter nostram salu tem	descen.

50
Et ex - spe - - - cto re - surrecti - o - nem mor - tu - o - - rum. Et vitam
Et ex - spe - - - cto re surrecti - o - nem. Et vitam ven -
Et ex - spe - - - cto re surrecti - o - nem mor - - tu - o - rum.
- o - nem mor - tu - o - rum. Et vi - tam ven - -
Et ex - spe - - - cto re surrectio - nem Et
60
ven - tu - ri sae - cu - li. A - - - - - - men, A - - - -
- tu - ri - sae - cu - li. A - - - - - - - men, A - - -
Et vitam ventu - ri saecu - li. A - - - men, A - - - - -
- - tu - - ri sae - - cu - - li. A - - -
vitam ven - tu - ri saeculi A - men, A - - - men, A -
- men, A - - - men, A - - - - - - - men.
- men, A - men, A - - - men.
- men, A - - - - - men A - - - - men, A - - - men.
- - - - - - - - men
- - - - - - - - - men, A - - - - - men.

Mass: Repleatur os meum laude.

Palestrina

50
- - lei - son, Chri - ste e - lei - - - - - son, Chri - ste e - -
- son, Christe e lei - son, Chri - - ste e - lei - son, Chri -
- lei son, Christe e - - lei - - son, Chri - ste e - lei - - -
Chri - - ste e - - lei - son, Christe e - lei - - son,
- lei - - - - - - - - - - - - son,
- - lei - son, Christe e - lei - - son, Chri - ste e - lei
- ste e - lei - - son, Christe e - lei - - - son,
son, Chri - ste e - - lei - son, Chri - ste e - lei - - - son,
Chri - ste e - lei - - - son,
Christe e - lei - son, Christe e - - - lei - - son, Chri -
60
- - son, Christe e - lei - - - - - - - - - son.
Christe e - lei - - - - - son.
Chri - ste e - lei - - - - son, Chri - ste e - lei - son.
Christe e - lei - - - - - son, Christe e - lai - - - - - son.
- ste e - lei - - - - son, Chri - ste e - lei - - son,

175

Sanctus

Resolutio
Canon ad Tertiam
San - ctus, ... San - - - - ctus, ... San - -
San - ctus, ... San - - - ctus, San -
San - -
10
- - ctus, San - - - - ctus, San - - ctus, Dominus De - us
- - ctus, San - - ctus Do - mi.nus De.us
San - - ctus, Sanctus, San - - - -
San - - ctus, San . ctus, San - - - - - ctus
- ctus, ... San - - ctus, San - - ctus, San - - ctus Do -
20
Sa - - ba - oth, Do. mi.nus Deus .... Sa - - ba . oth. Ple -
Sa. ba - - - oth, Dominus De - us Sa. ba - - oth, Do - minus De - us Sa -
ctus Do. minus De. us Sa - ba - - oth.
Dominus De. us Sa - ba - oth. Ple -
- minus De - us, Do - minus Deus Saba - oth, ... Sa - ba . oth..... Ple -

30
- ni sunt coeli et ter - ra, ple - ni sunt coe - li et ter - - - -
- ba - oth. Ple - ni sunt coe - li et ter - ra, ple - ni sunt coe - li et terra....
Ple - ni sunt coe - - li, ple - ni sunt coe -
- ni sunt coe - - li, ple - ni sunt coe - li et terra
- ni sunt coe - li et ter - ra, ple - ni sunt coe - li et ter - - - - -
- - - ra glori - a tu - - - - - a,..... glori - a tu - -
..... glo - ri - a tu - a, tu - - - - - - a, glo -
- li et ter - ra glori - a tu - - - a, glo - ri - a tu -
glo - ri - a tu - - - a, glori - a tu - - - a,
- - ra glo - ri - a..... tu - a, tu - - a, glori - a tu - - a, glo -
40
- a, glo - ri - a tu - - - a, glo - ri - a tu - - - a.
- ri - a tu - a, tu - - a, glo - - ri - a tu - a, tu - - - - a.
- - a, tu - - - - a.
tu - - - - - - - a.
- - ri - - - a tu - a, glo - ri - a tu - a, gloria......tu - a.

Agnus Dei. I.

CANTUS
ALTUS
TENOR(I)
QUINTUS TENOR(II)
BASSUS
Canon ad unisonam
Resolutio
A - gnus...... De - - - - i, qui tol - lis........
A - gnus De - - - - i,
A - gnus.......De - i,
A-gnus De - i, qui
A - - gnus......................De - - i,
A - gnus De - i A - -
10
....pec. ca - ta mun - di,
A - - gnus De - i, qui tol.lis pec.
A - gnus De - i, qui tollis.............. pec - ca - ta
tollis pec.ca - - ta mun - - - di:
A - gnus De - i, qui
-gnus De - i, qui tollis pec.ca.ta mun - - - di,........pec-

20
-ca-ta mun - - - di, ... mun - - di: mi-se-re-re no-
mun - - di: mi-se-re-re no - bis, mi-se - re-re no - bis, mi-
mi-se-re-re no - - bis, no - bis, ... mi-se-re-re ...
tol-lis pec-ca - - - ta mun - - - - - - -
-ca - ta mun - di: mi-se-re-re no - - bis, ...
- - - - bis, no - - - bis, mi-se-re - re no - - - -
-se - re - - re ... no - bis, mi-se-re - re no-bis, no - - -
no - bis, mi-se-re - re ... no - - bis, mi-se-re
- - - - di:
mi-se-re - - re no - - bis, mi - se-re-
30
- - bis, mi-se-re - re no - - - - - bis, ... mi-
- - bis, mi-se-re - re no - bis, mi-se-re-re ...
- re no - - - - - bis, mi-se-re - re no-bis, mi-se-re - - -
mi-se - re - - re no - - -
- - re no - bis, mi-se-re-re no-bis, ...

40
-sere. re .... no. bis, mi. se. re - - re no - - - - bis.
no - - bis, mi - se - re - re, mi. se. re - re no - - - bis.
-re no - - bis, mi. se. re - - - re no - - - - bis.
- bis, no - - - - bis.
mi - se. re - - re, mi. se. re - re no - - - - - bis.

Agnus Dei. II

Cantus II
Mezzo sopran.
A - gnus De - i, A - gnus De - - i,
A - gnus De - i, A. gnus De - - i, A - gnus De -
A - gnus De -

10
A - - - - - gnus De - - - - i,
A - - gnus De - i, A - gnus De - - -
A - - gnus De - i, A -
- - - i, A - - - - gnus...... De - - - -
-i, A - gnus De - - - - - i,
A - gnus De - - i, A - - gnus De - i, A - gnus De - - - i,

182

Orlandus Lassus (1532–1594)

Motet, *Tristis est anima mea*

[Note values halved]

189

My soul is exceedingly sorrowful, even unto death:
tarry ye here, and watch with me: now ye will see
the multitude that will surround me: ye will take
flight, and I shall go to be sacrificed for you.

Orlando di Lasso

Penitential Psalm III, v. 1, 10, 20

191

O Lord, rebuke me not in thy wrath: neither chasten me in thy
hot displeasure.
My heart panteth, my strength faileth me: as for the light of
my eyes, it also is gone from me.
They also that render evil for good are mine adversaries;
because I follow the thing that good is.   Psalm 38: 1, 10, 20

Giovanni Pierluigi da Palestrina (circa 1525–1594): Kyrie of the Mass „Assumpta est Maria"

Giovanni Palestrina (1525-1594)

Agnus Dei I

Missa Papae Marcelli

Mass: Ut Re Mi Fa Sol La: Kyrie

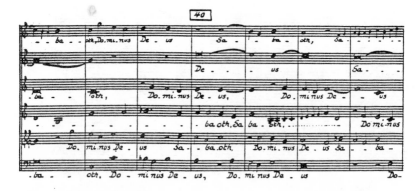

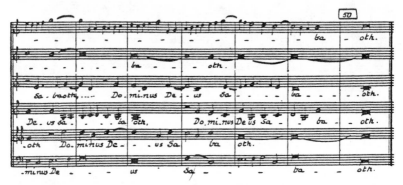

207

Motet: O admirabile commercium

Palestrina

208

20
ge - neris hu - ma - ni, a - ni-matum
ge-ne-ris hu-ma-ni, a-
ris hu-ma - - ni, a - ni-
ge - neris hu - ma - ni, a - ni-
a - ni - matum cor - - pus su - - mens,
a - nimatum cor - pus su - - - mens,
a - ni matum corpus su - - - - - - mens,
a - nimatum corpus su - - - - - - - mens,
corpus su - - - - - - mens, de Vir - gi - ne-
-ni-matum cor - pus su - mens, de Vir - gi - ne
matum cor - pus su - - mens, de Vir - - gi-ne
matum corpus su - - - - mens, de Vir - - gi - ne
de Vir - gi - ne na - sci
de Vir - gi - ne na - sci
de Vir - gi - ne na - sci
de Vir - gi - ne na - sci

et pro.cedens ho . mo si . ne se . mi . ne,
et pro.ce.dens ho . mo si . ne se . mi . ne,
et pro.ce . dens ho.mo ..... si.ne se.mi . ne,
et pro ce dens ho . mo si.ne se.mi . ne,
se mi. ne, lar. gi . tus est no . bis
. mi. ne, lar. gi.tus est no . bis
se mi ne, lar. gi.tus est no . bis
lar. gi . tus est no . bis
50
lar . gi . tus est no . bis su . am de . i . ta . tem
lar . gi . tus est no . bis su . am de . i ta . tem
lar. gi . tus est no . bis su. am de . i . ta . tem
lar. gi . tus est no . bis su . am de . i . ta . tem
su . am de . i . ta . tem lar . gi . tus est no . bis lar . gi . tus est
su . am de . i . ta . tem lar . gi . tus est no . bis lar . gi . tus est
su . am de . i . ta . tem lar . gi . tus est no . bis lar gi . tus est
su . am de . i . ta . tem lar . gi . tus est no . bis lar . gi . tus est

O wondrous exchange! The Creator of mankind,
taking upon himself a human body, has deigned
to be born of a virgin; and thus becoming man,
albeit without seed, he had made us sharers in
his divinity!

Motet: Laudate Dominum in tympanis

Palestrina.

Praise ye the Lord with timbrels, Sing ye unto the Lord with cymbals,
Sing unto him a new song! Exalt him and call upon his name!
For great and glorious is the Lord in his power,
The Lord who putteth an end to wars.
Sing a hymn to the Lord our God!

(From Judith XVI - 2,16,3,15.)

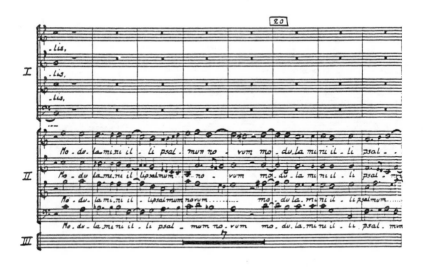

217